"Oh, Ryder, let me go," Ashley gasped. "I—"

"You respond to me when I kiss you, Ashley, you can't deny that. Why are you fighting what you're feeling?"

"I'm not. Well, all right, I am," she said, wiggling out of his arms. "I'm just not in the habit of kissing perfect strangers."

"Am I perfect?" he asked, grinning at her before taking a long, shuddering breath. "Whew! You really get to me, Ashley Ames. What did you do, whip up some magic potion from one of your plants?"

"Look, Cantrell, I mean, Ryder, this is crazy. We don't even know each other. You no doubt are used to getting whatever you want, and I'll admit I responded to your kisses, but there aren't going to be any more."

"We'll see." Ryder smiled, and Ashley felt herself start to weaken. Then she said firmly, "Cantrell, you are absolutely not to kiss me again. Get it?"

"Sure," he said, his smile deepening. Oh, he was going to kiss her again, he thought, no doubt about it. It was just going to call for a little strategy . . .

WHAT ARE *LOVESWEPT* ROMANCES?

They are stories of true romance and touching emotion. We believe those two very important ingredients are constants in our highly sensual and very believable stories in the *LOVESWEPT* line. Our goal is to give you, the reader, stories of consistently high quality that may sometimes make you laugh, sometimes make you cry, but are always fresh and creative and contain many delightful surprises within their pages.

Most romance fans read an enormous number of books. Those they truly love, they keep. Others may be traded with friends and soon forgotten. We hope that each *LOVESWEPT* romance will be a treasure—a "keeper." We will always try to publish

LOVE STORIES YOU'LL NEVER FORGET
BY AUTHORS YOU'LL ALWAYS REMEMBER

The Editors

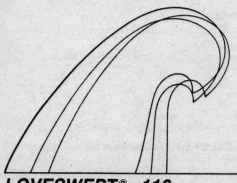

LOVESWEPT® • 116
Joan Elliott Pickart
Midnight Ryder

 BANTAM BOOKS
TORONTO • NEW YORK • LONDON • SYDNEY • AUCKLAND

MIDNIGHT RYDER

A Bantam Book / November 1985

*LOVESWEPT® and the wave device are registered
trademarks of Bantam Books, Inc. Registered in U.S. Patent
and Trademark Office and elsewhere.*

ISBN 0-553-21738-0

Published simultaneously in the United States and Canada

*Bantam Books are published by Bantam Books, Inc. Its
trademark, consisting of the words "Bantam Books" and
the portrayal of a rooster, is Registered in U.S. Patent and
Trademark Office and in other countries. Marca Registrada.
Bantam Books, Inc., 666 Fifth Avenue, New York, New
York 10103.*

PRINTED IN THE UNITED STATES OF AMERICA

O   0 9 8 7 6 5 4 3 2 1

*For Ryder, who became so real I hated
to write the last word and say good-bye.*

One

The man reached in the pocket of his blue western shirt and withdrew a pack of cigarettes, shaking
it and pulling one loose with his teeth. He replaced
the package and found a match next to it. He flicked
the tip with his thumbnail and cupped his hands to
shield the flame from the wind. Inhaling deeply, he
squinted against the rising smoke. The actions had
been executed absently, his mind elsewhere as he
performed the ritual.

He was a tall, handsome man, straight and taut,
shoulders wide and hips narrow. The shirt and jeans
he wore were faded and soft, molding themselves to
muscular thighs and corded arms. His skin was
deeply tanned, making his emerald eyes appear even
greener. His hair was thick and sandy-colored, falling
to the collar of his shirt and combed over his ears.

His gaze flickered over the scene before him,
encompassing all, missing no detail. He nodded
slightly in satisfaction. It was good, he thought, very

good. Nothing was once again becoming something, the old would be new, the ugliness replaced with beauty, of a sort. Yeah, it was good.

"Hey, Ryder!" a voice called.

"Yeah?" the man said, not turning his head in the direction of the summons.

"Phone!"

"Yeah." He took one last drag from the cigarette, then crushed it under the heel of his mud-splattered boots.

His long legs carried him to his destination in an easy, rolling gait. He had a limber, loose stride that might stand out, be noticed in a crowd somewhere else. But not there. Not in Texas.

Ryder pulled open the door to a trailer and entered, ducking his head, then straightening again as he picked the receiver up off the desk.

"Cantrell," he said, his voice deep, husky.

"Ryder? Lucy. You wanted me to call you when the letters went out."

"Damn. Yeah, okay. Listen, I'm not going to be able to get back there, like I planned. I don't want you taking any flak, and I intended to be around to run interference. Anyone hassles you, tell them to come out here and see me."

"All right. Who knows? Maybe they'll all consider you a hero."

He chuckled. "I doubt it. I'm usually cast as the villain. I'll check in later."

"Okay, Ryder."

Ryder replaced the receiver and pressed the heels of his hands to his eyes in a gesture of fatigue, then rotated his neck in an attempt to loosen the muscles, one large hand massaging his left shoulder.

"You're workin' too hard," a quiet voice said behind him, causing Ryder to spin around.

"Don't sneak up on me like that, Pappy," he growled.

"You're out on your feet, boy," the small, white-haired man said. "How far do you think you can push yourself?"

"Give it a rest, Pappy," Ryder said, reaching for his cigarettes and lighting one.

"It's your body that could use the rest, not my mouth. Are you hearing me, boy?"

"Yeah, yeah, I hear you."

"And?"

"Yeah, okay, I'll knock off early today. Go play mother to somebody else for a while."

"I'll be circling back later to see that you've gone home. I mean it, Ryder—you're burnin' yourself out."

"I'm thirty-seven years old, Pappy, not eighty-seven. I've got a few breaths left in me."

"Not for long, you haven't, at the rate you're goin'," Pappy said, leaving the trailer.

Ryder scowled at the little man's retreating back, then ground out the cigarette in an overflowing ashtray. Maybe he *would* go home early today, he thought. He was tired, bone weary, and if he didn't lighten up he was going to start making mistakes.

Ryder Cantrell did *not* like to make mistakes.

"Ryder?" a man said, sticking his head in the door. "Can you come down and check those footings?"

"Yeah, I'm coming," he answered, lifting a Stetson off a peg on the wall and putting it on.

Ashley looked up as the door to the warehouse opened and the mailman entered.

"Ashley Hunt?" the man said.

"Yes."

"Sign here, please. Registered letter, special delivery."

"For me?"

"Yes, ma'am. Come into our office an hour ago, and now you've got it. How's that for service?"

"Impressive," she said as she signed the receipt. "I've never gotten one of these before."

"Hope it's good news," the mailman said as he went back out the door.

Ashley flipped a heavy dark braid over her shoulder as she stared at the envelope in her hand.

"Cantrell Construction," she read aloud from the corner of the beige envelope. "Never heard of them. Well, open it."

She slid a fingertip under the flap and withdrew the letter. She flicked it open and read it quickly, her eyes widening as the words struck her like a physical blow. The air seemed to swoosh from her lungs, leaving her breathless, panting, as tiny black spots swirled in front of her eyes. Her hand flew to her mouth to muffle the cry that escaped, and the trembling in her legs forced her to grab a chair and sink into it heavily.

"No!" she said, staring at the paper clutched tightly in her hand. "No, no!" This wasn't happening to her! It was a joke. Yes, yes, a joke. That crazy Josh had . . . But the letterhead looked authentic.

Ashley yanked open the desk drawer and pulled out the telephone book, flipping frantically through the pages. There it was. Cantrell Construction. It could still be a hoax, she assured herself. Cantrell Whoever could be in on it with Josh. If it was a prank, he would wring Josh's neck. If not? If not . . .

"Over my dead body, Cantrell!" she said, jumping o her feet and stalking to the door.

The fear was gone. The horror, the shock, the icy

chill, were replaced by rage. Red-hot, rip-roaring anger.

Ashley retraced her steps, tugged her purse from the desk drawer, and left the warehouse. She climbed into the driver's seat of her ancient brown van and roared the engine into action. A few minutes later she was whipping through the Houston traffic, oblivious to the cool April weather and the blue sky dotted with fluffy clouds.

Ashley Hunt had only one thought.

Cantrell.

At a red light, she picked the crumpled letter up off the seat and double-checked the address. It was on San Jacinto Street, downtown, where the tall office buildings towered above the city, poking their peaks into the heavens. Ashley's glance fell on the slash of ink that was the signature, and the neatly typed name and title below. Ryder Cantrell, President.

"Ryder?" she muttered, pressing on the gas pedal as the light turned green. "It has to be phony. It's so macho-sounding, it's sick. No one really has a name like Ryder Cantrell, does he? Does he? Oh-h-h, I hope this is a joke."

She knew the building would be there, because, after all, it had been listed in the telephone book. And the fact that Cantrell Construction was shown on the lobby directory as being on the tenth floor was acceptable, as it was obvious that Cantrell *did* exist. The clincher was whether or not Ryder Cantrell was in cahoots with Josh.

The reception area of Cantrell Construction was plush and expensively furnished, and the beautiful woman behind the desk smiled warmly at Ashley.

"Hello, my name is Lucy. May I help you?" she said.

"I need to see Cantrell. Ryder Cantrell."

"Ryder is out of the office. Would you like to make an appointment for another time?"

"No, it's imperative that I . . . The jig is up, you know."

"I beg your pardon?"

"The joke, the con, between Josh and Cantrell. I've received the letter and, believe me, I don't find this one bit humorous."

"I'm afraid I don't understand, Miss . . ."

"Ashley Hunt."

"Oh, yes, I remember typing your letter. I know that this must have come as a shock to you, Miss Hunt, and I'm sorry. However, there's nothing that can be done."

Ashley ran her tongue nervously over her lips and stared intently at Lucy's face. It was true, she thought. Oh, dear heaven, it was true! The sympathetic tone of Lucy's voice, the concern radiating from her green eyes, left no doubt in Ashley's mind as to the validity of the letter. This wasn't a hoax, it was a nightmare!

"I must see Cantrell," Ashley said, ignoring the trembling of her own voice. "Now!"

"It won't help, Miss Hunt. You'll only upset yourself more and—"

"Where is he?" Ashley said, her anger mounting again. "Is he hiding under a rock, like the snake that he is? What kind of man would do something like this? Has he no conscience, no morals, no heart?"

"I—"

"Where is that reprobate?"

"Reprobate?" Lucy said, her eyes widening as a giggle escaped from her lips. "I don't think I've ever heard him called that before."

"Well, he is! And a scoundrel, and a—a blackguard!"

"Oh, good Lord." Lucy dissolved into a fit of

laughter. "I love it. Here," she said, scribbling on a piece of paper. "Ryder is at this address."

"Thank you," Ashley said primly. "Lucy, is it?"

"Cantrell." She grinned. "Lucy Cantrell."

"You're . . . Oh, I'm sorry! I . . . Oh-h-h," Ashley said, spinning around and dashing from the office, her cheeks crimson with embarrassment.

"Why do I miss all the good stuff?" Lucy said with a moan. "I'd give ten bucks to be out on that job site when Ashley Hunt shows up."

And show up she did.

With braids flapping against her back and a murderous expression on her face she stomped across the muddy ground and confronted the first person she saw. Pappy.

"I want to see Cantrell!" Ashley demanded.

"Do you, now?" Pappy said. "I take it this isn't a social call?"

"Hardly! Where is the crumb?"

"Missy, why don't you just calm yourself down a bit here and—"

"Don't try to sweet-talk me! I'll comb every inch of this place until I find him!"

"Okay, you win. Come along."

Ashley splashed her way through the puddles as she walked behind the old man, and nearly skidded into him when he came to an abrupt halt.

"He's over there." Pappy pointed to five men who were standing close together, obviously deeply engrossed in conversation.

"Thank you." She marched past Poppy.

"This area should be staked by tomorrow," one of the men was saying as Ashley approached.

"Cantrell," she said.

"This section," the man continued, pointing to a paper in his hand, "is scheduled for—"

"*Cantrell!*" Ashley shrieked.

Silence.

As if in slow motion, the five big men turned and stared at Ashley, who planted her hands on her hips and glowered. Suddenly the tallest of the group took three long strides forward, shoved his Stetson back with his thumb, and frowned down at Ashley from his lofty height.

"I'm Cantrell," he said, his voice seeming to rumble up the entire rugged length of him.

It fit, Ashley thought wildly. The name Ryder Cantrell fit this man! He was the most masculine specimen she had ever seen in her life. Every muscled, gorgeous inch of him shouted virility, announced a blatant sexuality that was absolutely scrumptious. Was she nuts? she asked herself. This was Cantrell! The enemy!

"Well?" he asked, his gaze sweeping over her slender figure, clad in pink bib overalls. She was small, he noted, couldn't be more than five feet four, and pretty, with a natural, healthy glow to her skin. She was also, he mused, mad as hell about something.

"I want to talk to you," she said tightly.

"So, talk."

"In private."

"Does your mother know you're out?" he asked, eliciting a whoop of laughter from the men behind him.

"Don't push me, Cantrell!"

"Or what?" He smiled, his white teeth flashing against tanned skin. "You'll deck me?"

Oh, sweet heaven, Ashley thought, what a beautiful smile. It had just swept across that unbelievable face.

"I'm a busy man," Cantrell went on. "If you have something to say, say it."

She looked up into Ryder Cantrell's emerald eyes

and saw no warmth there, no gentleness. A flicker of amusement was evident, but that was all. The men behind him were obviously enjoying the performance, and she could see the old man she had first spoken to was inching closer, so as not to miss any of the scene. She was definitely doing nothing more than making a spectacle of herself, so she would change her tactics.

"Well"—she sighed—"if you insist on my speaking right here in front of these men, I guess I'll have to."

"I insist," Cantrell said.

"Well, then, darlin'," Ashley said, ever so sweetly, "I just can't go another day without that money you promised me so I can buy milk for our starving baby boy. Our son is so-o-o hungry and I—"

"That's it!" Contrell growled, grabbing her by the arm and starting off across the muddy expanse with her in tow. The men's hoots and hollers were immediately quelled by the stormy glare Ryder threw back over his shoulder.

Ashley scrambled to keep up with the long-legged stride of Ryder Cantrell and realized she was nearly airborne as he propelled her forward and deposited her none too gently inside a trailer. He yanked the door closed behind him and plopped her in a chair. His hat was thrown roughly onto a small sofa. Then he turned and gripped the arms of the chair, bending over and speaking only inches from Ashley's startled face.

"Who in the hell are you, kid?" he ground out.

Never, ever in her days on earth had she seen such an angry man. His eyes were emerald daggers. A muscle was twitching in his rugged jaw and a pulse was beating wildly in the strong column of his neck. Ashley had the irrational thought that her next breath would be her last. She was a dead person!

"I," she croaked, "am not a kid!"

Cantrell's shoulders slumped, and he bent his head as if mentally counting to ten. Ashley's gaze was riveted on the thick crop of sandy-colored hair filling her entire line of vision. It was actually, she decided, several different shades, almost blond in parts. It appeared silky and oh, so inviting, as if screaming at her to run her fingers through its softness. He smelled good, too. An all-mixed-up aroma of fresh air, and male perspiration, and cigarettes. Sweat and tobacco should have been offensive, but on Ryder Cantrell they were totally male.

"Okay," he said, taking a deep breath and pushing himself away from the chair. "Let's try again. Who are you?"

"Ashley Hunt."

"And you're claiming to have had my baby?"

"No, of course not!" she snapped. "I was simply trying to get your attention."

"Oh, you got it, all right," he said, resting on the edge of the desk and crossing his long legs at the ankles.

Her gaze flickered over the faded material of Cantrell's jeans. She saw the bunching muscles of his thighs beneath the soft fabric, and felt a strange fluttering sensation in the pit of her stomach.

"See something you want?" he asked dryly.

"What?" she said, her gaze flying to his face as her cheeks burned with heat. "Listen, Cantrell, don't get crude."

"Me? You're the person giving me the once-over. That can get you in a lot of trouble, little girl."

"I am not a—"

"Yeah, okay, fine. Would you just state your business and be on your way? I have work to do, which does not include baby-sitting pig-tailed brats in pink overalls."

"You are despicable!" she said, jumping to her feet. "I am twenty-five years old, you dimwit, and I demand to be treated with respect."

"Well, la-di-da," he said.

"Lord, I despise you!"

"What in the hell did I do to you?" he bellowed, making her jump.

"You're a . . . a building killer, a life wrecker, a dream destroyer, a—"

"Hold it!" he said, raising his hand.

"I won't stand for it, Cantrell! You won't get away with this. You can send me a fancy letter every day for the next fifty years, and it won't mean a thing."

"Oh, I see." He nodded. "So that's what this is all about. You got one of the letters."

"Yes!" she said, yanking it out of her purse and waving it in the air. "But you can forget it. As far as I'm concerned I never saw this thing and—"

"Miss Hunt," he said quietly, "there's nothing you can do."

"There has to be. You don't understand. Don't do this to me, Cantrell."

"Dammit." He walked over to her and gripped her by the shoulders. "It's not me. I'm just the guy who won the bid on the contract."

"Then refuse to do it!"

"If it isn't me, it will be someone else. The letter explained it. We're talking about eminent domain here. In this country the state can take possession of any property for the benefit of the majority. The university has proclaimed that that area, including your property, is needed for the expansion of the campus. The majority, in this case, is thousands of students who will benefit from the additions. The land will be cleared and new buildings constructed. You can't stop it. You'll get a fair, assessed price."

"No. Oh, no," she said, tears filling her eyes.

Oh, man, Ryder thought, look at her face. Tears. He'd never dealt with a reaction like Ashley's. Anger and threats, yes, but never tears from a heartbroken little whisper of a girl. No, she was a woman. A frightened, shaken woman. Lord, what was he going to do with her?

"Ashley, don't cry," he said gently. "This has all hit you very quickly, but once you calm down you'll see that—"

"You really don't care, do you?" she asked, backing away from him. "It's just another job to you. It doesn't matter that you're destroying everything I've worked so hard for."

"You'll have the funds to go somewhere else."

"I'm barely scraping by now! My warehouse isn't only where I run my business, but where I live. Everything I have is wrapped up in that place."

"You live in a warehouse?"

"I can't afford an apartment. I'm not going to get much money for that building. It's old and not in such great shape, but it's perfect for me. I'll never find anything even close to it that I can afford. Oh, please, Cantrell, help me stop these people."

A single tear slid down Ashley's cheek, and Ryder felt as though someone had punched him in the stomach. He walked over to her and cupped her face in his large hands, brushing the tear away with his thumb. Their eyes met and held in a timeless moment, and then slowly, slowly he lowered his head and kissed her.

He hadn't intended to kiss her. He simply did it. His tongue slid over her lips, seeking and gaining entry to the inner darkness of her mouth. The kiss intensified as he gathered Ashley close to his chest, crushing her breasts against him. Somewhere in the back of his mind Ryder knew he was making a mistake. A very big mistake. And as equally crystal-clear was the knowledge that it was too late to do a damn thing about it.

Ashley was swept away on a wave of sensations as Ryder's soft, sensuous lips seemed to draw the breath from her body. She molded herself to him, allowing her body to be fitted against his hard contours as their tongues met. Shock waves of desire rocketed through her. She had never responded to a man's kiss like this, and it was ecstasy. Ryder Cantrell was like none before. He was the ultimate of masculinity in a six-foot-plus package and he was kissing *her*. He was also married!

"Oh, dear heaven." Ashley gasped, jerking free of Ryder's embrace.

"What?" he said, looking at her a little dazedly.

"How dare you!" she yelled. "Have you no scruples? Don't you place one ounce of importance on the vows you took?"

"Huh?"

"Of course you don't! What would I expect from a building killer?"

"I don't know what's got you all fired up, lady, but you kissed me back!"

"You started it! Shame on you. I met your Lucy. How can you be unfaithful to such a sweet person?"

"Lucy?"

"Lucy Cantrell? Your wife? Surely you remember her. You are a cad! Yes, that's a great word. A despicable cad."

"Lucy?" Ryder said, whooping with laughter. "You think Lucy is—"

"Shut up, Cantrell. I won't stand here and listen to you say derogatory things about—"

"My sister!"

"I beg your pardon?"

"Lucy Cantrell is my sister, Miss High-and-Mighty."

"Oh," Ashley said quietly. "Fancy that."

"Which leaves me free to kiss whomever I damn well please. Now that my innocence has been determined, shall we discuss your part in our passionate exchange?"

"It was *not* passionate. Well, it sort of was. But you snuck up on me when I was in a weakened emotional state."

"I see," he said, grinning at her. "If that was weakened, I'd love to see you at full tilt."

"Stuff it, Cantrell. This conversation is ridiculous."

"My name is Ryder," he said, his voice low. "Ryder."

"Cantrell," she said, "I am here to discuss the fact that you are about to demolish my warehouse, my home, my future. . . ."

"Ashley," he said, raking his hand through his hair, "there is nothing, *nothing* I can do."

"I'll go to the Board of Regents at the university."

"No. Look, those letters usually come from the institution invoking the eminent-domain law. In my bid I stipulated that everything goes through me. You're wasting your time going to the university, anyway. Their minds are made up."

"Do you get some kind of perverse pleasure out of being the hatchet man?"

"It just saves a lot of hassle. I once did an eminent-domain contract in Dallas, and those people went through every university official they could find, while I stood around trying to get the project going. It's simpler this way. I send out the letters, take the flak, and get the show on the road."

"I'm going to fight this, Cantrell."

"You can't win. You have thirty days to relocate. Use the time constructively. Find a new place to house whatever it is you've got in that warehouse and accept things as they are."

"No!"

"Hell!" He reached into his pocket for a cigarette and lit it.

The two stood glaring at each other, the air in the small room seeming to crackle with tension. Then Ashley ran her tongue over her lips, drew a shuddering breath, and sank onto a chair.

"Are you all right?" Ryder asked quietly.

"You shouldn't smoke, you know," she said, getting slowly to her feet. "It's bad for your health."

"Ashley . . ."

"I'm sorry for the scene I caused. I'll get out of your way now. Good-bye, Cantrell," she said, walking to the door.

"Ashley?"

"Yes?"

"It's Ryder."

"Good-bye . . . Ryder." She closed the door quietly behind her.

Ryder brought the cigarette to his lips, then snuffed it out in the ashtray instead. Shoving his hands into his back pockets, he stared at the door Ashley Hunt had gone through, a deep frown creasing his brow. He was still standing there a few minutes later, when Pappy entered the trailer.

"Looks like you had your hands full with that little gal," Pappy said. "What was she all in a dither about?"

"She's caught in the eminent-domain contract."

"She looked mighty dejected when she left, as if all the fight had gone out of her."

"Dammit, it's not my fault!" Ryder roared, causing Pappy to look at him in surprise. "I'm just the hired help. I'm not the one taking away everything she's got and making her cry. I— Forget it. She's not my problem."

"Of course she isn't," Pappy said calmly. "Besides, she seems like the type who can take care of herself."

"Are you nuts? She's living in that warehouse I'm about to plow under. You saw her. She's no bigger than a minute, and— Ah, hell!" Ryder snatched up his Stetson and stalked out of the trailer.

"Well, well, well," Pappy said merrily. "Now, *this* could get interesting."

Ryder scowled as he strode across the muddy ground, lighting a cigarette as he went. Ashley Hunt could take care of herself? Ha! he thought fiercely. What a joke. Granted, she'd come barreling in there and taken him on like a storm trooper, but then? Lord, when those big brown eyes of hers had filled with tears he'd felt awful. Why in the hell had he kissed her? But what a kiss it had been. There was a passionate woman beneath the pigtails and pink overalls. A very passionate woman.

Ah, hell, why was he worrying about her? he asked himself. He hadn't caused her to cry. He wasn't the one yanking the props out from under her. She'd have to toughen up and accept the facts as they were. She was no different from anyone else who'd ever been uprooted by the eminent-domain law. Ashley Hunt *was not his problem!*

Ryder flicked the cigarette into a puddle and absently massaged his left shoulder as he scanned the construction work in progress. The condos would look sharp, he thought, be a vast improvement over the trash-filled empty lots that had been an eyesore. People would have decent places to live. Where was Ashley going to live when he creamed her warehouse?

"That's it," he muttered under his breath. "Enough of her. Hank!" he yelled.

"Yeah, boss?"

"Take over. I'm going back to the office."

"Yo!"

"And then home early?" Pappy asked.

"Don't sneak up on me!" Ryder bellowed as he strode away, leaving Pappy grinning at his retreating back.

Ashley hardly remembered driving back to the warehouse. She was just there suddenly, flinging herself across the bed and sobbing into her pillow. She cried until there were no more tears, and then she lay huddled in misery, curled up in a ball.

That was how Josh found her.

"Ashley? What's wrong?" he asked, settling down on the edge of the bed.

"Oh, Josh," she said, sitting up and flinging her arms around his neck. "Josh."

"Hey, take it easy," he said, prying her loose and looking at her tear-stained face. "Calm down and tell me what's going on."

Joshua Emery Smith was twenty-one years old, a senior in college, majoring in business and minoring in body building and women. He strutted his stuff, considered himself extremely handsome, with his curly black hair and muscle-bound body, and loved Ashley like a brother. They had met a year before, when Ashley had purchased the warehouse and discovered that Josh was living illegally in the empty building.

Ashley had agreed to let Josh stay for one week, until he could find somewhere else to sleep, but he had never gotten around to leaving. He had become the muscle behind Ashley's brain and helped convert the warehouse into the efficient operation it was now. Josh was a whiz with a hammer and saw and had constructed two bedrooms in the building, along with the tiny kitchen and bathroom that they shared.

Ashley paid him a small salary and gave him room and board for his ongoing labor in the slowly growing business, and they were both pleased with the arrangement.

They respected each other's privacy, and Josh never brought any of his women to the warehouse. He simply disappeared most weekends, and Ashley asked no questions. They had something together that they treasured. They were friends.

"Ashley, talk to me," Josh said.

"It's over, Josh," she said, taking a shuddering breath. "Finished."

"What are you talking about?"

"Read that letter sticking out of my purse."

Josh grabbed the crumpled paper and scanned it quickly.

"Like hell!" he said, jumping to his feet. "No way! Nobody's coming in here and— I'll go find this scum Cantrell and beat him to a pulp. That ought to be a clear enough answer to this crap."

"No, Josh, it's useless. I've seen Cantrell. It's not his fault. The university is evoking the eminent-domain law. There's nothing we can do."

"There has to be something, some way to stop this, Ashley."

"There isn't," she said softly. "We have thirty days to get out."

"And go where?"

"I don't know. They'll assess the building and pay for it."

"Wonderful. This place is worthless."

"It's all I have, Josh."

"What's this Cantrell dude like?"

Ashley looked up quickly at Josh as the image of Ryder Cantrell flashed before her eyes. Ryder? she thought. Ryder was like no man she had ever met before. He was an enigma, his personality seeming to possess many facets. His eyes had glinted like cold chips of jade, then softened with warmth and tenderness. He emanated sexuality simply by being there. He didn't flaunt himself with youthful cockiness like Josh, but moved with self-assurance, unspoken authority. His body was taut, strong, yet he had tempered his strength with gentleness when he held her in his arms. He had kissed her with practiced expertise and evoked passions within her she had not known she was capable of feeling. What kind of man was Ryder Cantrell? She really didn't know.

"Ashley, where are you?"

"What? I'm sorry, Josh. I'm just so bummed out. Cantrell isn't important. He's the contractor hired to do the job, that's all. Oh, Josh, it's useless. There's no one to fight, nothing we can do. I can't even think straight right now. We'll talk later when I can string two sentences together without crying, okay?"

"You just want me to leave you alone for a while?"

"Yes. Yes, please."

"All right, sweetheart," he said, kissing her on the forehead. "I'll see you later. In the meantime I'll put my superior mind to work on this and find a genius-level solution. Worry not, your Josh is leaping into action."

"What can I say?" Ashley smiled. "My troubles are over."

"You betcha. 'Bye."

Ashley sank back against the pillows and closed her eyes, pressing her hands to her aching temples. Josh was dear and sweet, and she adored him. He could not, however, make the bad guys go away by simply flexing his muscles. How quickly life could change. The simplest thing could bring major upheavals. A telephone call, a letter, a kiss, were capable of . . . A kiss? Where had that thought come from? Ryder.

Ashley brushed her fingertips over her lips and felt a tingling that started in the pit of her stomach and traveled throughout her. The sight, the feel, the aroma, the very essence of Ryder Cantrell seemed to assault her. Her breasts grew taut beneath her cotton T-shirt, and she sat up quickly as a flush of warmth crept onto her cheeks.

"Good heavens," she said, "what is it about that man? Go away, Cantrell. I have enough on my mind!"

Ryder entered the office and stopped at Lucy's desk, picking up the messages she had stacked neatly in a pile. He leafed through them and tossed them back in a heap.

"Hello to you too," Lucy said.

"Sorry. I was thinking about something. Everything all right here?"

"Fine. How're things at the site?"

"The usual."

"Nothing exciting happen? Say, for example, like a visit from a very irate girl in pink overalls?"

"Yeah, she came ready to shoot me on sight."

"Did you calm her down?"

He frowned, reaching for his cigarettes. "She cried, Lucy. She screamed and hollered and then she cried."

"Oh, Ryder, how awful. I feel so sorry for her. She's so young."

"She's five years younger than you are. Ashley's no kid, Lucy."

"Ashley? You're on a first-name basis?"

"Not exactly. Was there anything on her address to indicate what she does in that damn warehouse of hers besides live there?"

"She lives in a warehouse?"

"Where's the copy of the letter?"

"Right here. Let's see. Miss Ashley Hunt. Plants-to-Go."

"Plants?"

"To-Go."

"Go where?"

"Wait a minute, Ryder. I've heard of that outfit. My friend Susie uses them for her beauty shop. Ashley brings in plants for decoration and then comes back regularly to care for them. That way, businesses have attractive greenery without the hassle of fussing with them. It's a very good idea. Your Ashley is no dummy."

"She is not mine!"

"Figure of speech. Can't she just find another building?"

"She says her place isn't worth much, plus she lives there to cut down expenses."

"What's going to happen to her?"

"I don't know," he said, massaging his shoulder.

"Ryder, you're exhausted. Even your shoulder is bothering you. You're working much too hard. Why don't you go home and get some rest?"

"Are *you* going to start in on me now? Pappy's been jumping my butt all day."

"We love you, Ryder," Lucy said. "We don't like to see you driving yourself this way."

"I'm a big boy. I can watch out for myself," he said roughly.

"Can you? Prove it. Go home. Have a decent meal and get a lot of sleep. Oh, Ryder, you have enough money to last a lifetime and you don't enjoy any of it. You're a man, not a machine. You can't go on like this. You haven't even been out to the ranch in weeks."

"You've made your point, Lucy."

"And?"

"Okay! I've got some plans to look over. I'll knock off in about an hour."

"Good. Ryder? What's going to become of Ashley Hunt?"

"How should I know?" he asked, starting off down the hall. "I'm not her keeper!"

"It's a lucky thing for her that you're not!" Lucy called after him. "You can't even take care of yourself!"

Naggy woman, Ryder thought, tossing his Stetson onto a chair in his office. Everyone had a mother complex these days. Lucy had a lot of gall to insinuate he couldn't take proper care of a woman like Ashley Hunt. If Ashley were his, she'd sure as hell never cry again. Never. Plants-to-Go, he mused. Dumb name. Not a bad concept, though. Ashley obviously had a brain in that pretty head of hers. Hell, she'd be all right. Wouldn't she?

Ryder sat down on the soft leather sofa with a sigh and leaned his head back, shutting his eyes.

An instant later he was asleep.

Two

Ryder stirred, and groaned as he felt the stiff muscles in his neck. The room was pitch-black, and he blinked in confusion. Pushing himself to his feet, he made his way to his desk and turned on the lamp. As light flooded the room he glanced at his watch.

Ten o'clock. Damn, he thought. He'd have Lucy's hide for letting him sleep for hours. He was hungry, *starving*, and needed a shower. Lucy Cantrell was going to hear about this!

A few minutes later, Ryder emerged from the building and climbed behind the wheel of his late-model pickup truck. He drove across town to the high-rise apartment building he lived in and was soon entering his living room. Massive dark wood furniture upholstered in tones of brown, tan, and orange made the room masculine but inviting. Ryder strode into the bedroom, stripped off his clothes, and headed for the shower. Afterward, re-dressed in jeans and a clean western shirt, he consumed three ham sandwiches and a quart of milk. When he settled onto the sofa, he was wide awake.

Wonderful, he thought. Now he'd probably prowl around half the night, unable to sleep. Lucy had a lot of nerve, going off and leaving him in the office like that.

He glanced around the room and wondered absently what the place would look like with some plants in it. Plants-to-Go. Ashley. There she was again, creeping into his mind. Had she calmed down? Was she sleeping peacefully, ready to face tomorrow with a determination to make the best of her new situation? Or was she crying?

She was crying.

Ashley hadn't been able to sleep, so she was wandering through the long, neat rows of healthy, growing plants. She ran her fingertip over shiny leaves, drank in the aroma of fragrant blossoms, and cried. She cried because she wanted to, because there was no reason to stop. Her tears, she decided, were like raindrops, falling slowly, gently, unobtrusively. Rain cleansed the air and sky and ground. Her tears were for her heart and mind and soul. Rain washed the dust away and started everything new, fresh, and sparkling. Her tears would erase the memories, the dreams and hopes, and leave her free to begin again. And she would. Somehow.

But for now, she cried.

Josh was gone when she woke late the next morning. She had heard him moving around the kitchen the previous night, but had stayed in her room, not wishing to discuss the situation. She ate a quick breakfast and then checked her log book to see which plants at various businesses needed her attention. She jotted down her agenda and headed out the door.

* * *

Ryder stalked into the office, braced his hands flat on Lucy's desk, put his face an inch from hers, and scowled at her.

"You're fired," he said.

"Have a nice nap, Ryder, dear?"

"Dammit, Lucy, I didn't wake up until ten o'clock!"

"Tsk, tsk. That should show you how tired you were. Have a cup of coffee. It'll improve your mood."

"I said you are fired!"

"Oh, hush. You're bellowing like a wounded bull."

"Women!" Ryder said, stalking down the hall as Lucy dissolved in a fit of laughter.

Ryder spent the next hour on the telephone checking details with his foremen on various job sites around the city, as well as one in Austin and another outside of San Antonio. Everything was running smoothly. He tossed his pen onto the desk, then laced his fingers behind his head and stared at the ceiling as he leaned back in his chair.

He had not seen the property claimed in the eminent-domain contract, he thought. He'd sent his top man to analyze the situation and calculate the bid. Maybe he should drive over and see what was going to be involved in clearing the land. The present occupants had thirty days in which to vacate, but he liked to be one step ahead of things. He decided he'd go have a look around.

Ryder stood up and glanced around his office. No plants, he thought. Why hadn't he ever noticed that before?

"I'll call in," he said as he passed Lucy's desk.

"Where are you going?"

"Out!"

"Ta-ta, Mr. Sunshine," she said, waggling her fingers at him.

"You're fired, Lucy!"

When Ashley returned to the warehouse, Josh was in the kitchen, with his nose buried in a book and a large stack of other volumes in front of him.

"Hi," she said. "Studying hard?"

"I'm looking up everything I can find on eminent domain."

"And?"

"We're dead meat."

"I tried to tell you that, Josh."

He sighed. "I know, but I was hoping to come across a loophole. Ashley, I can always find a place to live for the couple of months until I graduate. It's you I'm worried about."

"I— There's the bell. Someone just came in. I'll go."

Ashley flipped her single braid to her back and smoothed her red terry-cloth top over the waistband of her jeans as she walked into the main area of the warehouse.

"Cantrell," she gasped. "What are you doing here?"

"The name is Ryder," he said, pushing his Stetson back with his thumb.

His shirt matched his eyes, Ashley thought distractedly. It did! Green, green, green. The jeans were newer than yesterday's, but still molded themselves like a glove to that body. But why was he here?

"Somehow I get the feeling you didn't come to buy a plant," she said coolly.

"This is quite an operation you have here," he remarked, walking slowly forward. He quickly assessed the low-hanging fluorescent lights suspended from the ceiling and the rows of growing troughs. "Nice job."

"It's neat as a pin and ready for you to smash to smithereens."

"Ashley, I—"

"I'm sorry. That wasn't fair. I know none of this is your fault, Cantrell. It's just easy to lash out at you because your name was on the letter. I've accepted what's happening."

"Do you know what you're going to do?" he asked.

"No, not really. It's taken me all these hours to calm down and resign myself to the inevitable. Are you here to see how the building is constructed or something?"

Ryder looked down at Ashley, at her big brown eyes, her small, firm breasts, her gently sloping hips. No, he hadn't come to see the warehouse. He'd probably known that when he left his office. But he wasn't about to tell Ashley Hunt he'd driven clear across town to make sure she wasn't crying!

"Yeah." He spoke gruffly.

"Well, help yourself," she said, waving a hand in the air.

"It can keep. I don't want to upset you by walking around like a potential executioner."

Ashley smiled. "You're reminding me that I called you a building killer. Seems I owe you quite a few apologies."

"No, you don't. Not at all. I'm not blaming you for your reaction to this thing. Besides, our meeting yesterday was not all bad, as I recall. That kiss we shared was very memorable."

"Kiss?" she repeated, raising her eyebrows. "I don't remember any kiss. I blank out sometimes when I'm distressed." Oh, dear heaven, she thought, her cheeks were warm. She wasn't blushing, was she? She'd die if she were!

"Then why are you blushing?" Ryder asked, grinning at her. Lord, she was cute, he thought. Absolutely adorable. And he wanted to kiss her again. Now! She had felt like a fragile china doll in his arms, had made him acutely aware of his own strength. But he'd never hurt her. Never. He'd be tender, gentle, and . . .

Ashley suddenly realized that Ryder was no longer smiling. He was gazing directly into her eyes, and the expression on his face was unreadable. She felt mesmerized by his emerald eyes, held by some magical spell, unable to move. Her heart was beating wildly and excitement was dancing up her spine.

"Ashley!" Josh called.

"Oh, Lord." She jumped in surprise. She turned to see Josh walking toward her.

"I'm going to take these books back to the library," Josh said.

"Okay. Oh, Josh Smith, this is Ryder Cantrell."

"Cantrell?" Josh frowned. "You're the dude who's tearing down this building?"

"Josh, don't," Ashley said. "You know it's not his fault."

"Yeah, well, I'd feel better if I broke his jaw," Josh answered.

"You're welcome to try." Ryder pulled his Stetson firmly forward on his head. "Got your insurance paid up, kid?"

"Oh, for Pete's sake," Ashley said, planting her hands on her hips. "You sound like little boys on the playground."

"Your buddy, here, has delusions of grandeur," Ryder said.

"I'll make mincemeat out of you, Cantrell," Josh shouted.

"You're getting on my nerves, kid," Ryder warned, his voice ominously low.

"Josh, go to the library," Ashley ordered.

"Like hell I will. I'm not leaving you here with him!"

Ryder made a noise that could only be defined as a snort and crossed his arms over the broad expanse of his chest. He spread his legs slightly and stared at Josh, who unconsciously took a half step backward. The two men glared at each other for a long moment, then Josh spun on his heel and stalked out of the warehouse without another word.

"Who was that muscle-bound twit?" Ryder growled.

"He lives here."

"What? Here? With you?"

"Yes. Well, no, not exactly."

"Ashley, are you sleeping with that flea brain?" Ryder yelled. Hell, what difference did it make? he wondered. It was none of his business but, dammit, the idea of Ashley and that—

"Josh is my friend," she said, interrupting his thoughts. "Besides, what gives you the right to ask me such a question? Whom I do or do not sleep with is none of your concern."

"He's your friend? How cozy. Maybe your lover would be interested in knowing about our kiss yesterday."

"Josh is not my lover!"

"And Lucy is not my wife," Ryder said, closing the distance between them. "So that leaves us both free to . . ."

The kiss was soft and sensuous in the beginning, then intensified as Ryder gathered Ashley close to his chest and parted her lips with his tongue. Fingers of desire crept through her, and she leaned heavily against Ryder's rugged length.

Again Ryder had the fleeting thought that kissing Ashley Hunt was a mistake. And again he ignored the small voice in his mind. She was heaven itself in his arms, her mouth a honeyed warmth, and he did *not* want to end the searing embrace.

Ashley drank in the male aroma of Ryder Cantrell and relished the feel of his taut body pressing against hers. His kiss, his touch were sweeping her into oblivion, away from reality and reason.

As his large hands slid down over her hips and pulled her up tight against him, the evidence of his arousal made her inwardly rejoice that this incredibly virile man wanted her. Her!

When Ryder finally lifted his head, she saw the smoky haze of desire in his emerald eyes. Suddenly she remembered how cold those eyes could be, how filled with anger. Ryder Cantrell was many men, none of whom she really knew.

"Cantrell," she gasped.

"Ryder," he said, his lips still close to hers.

"Oh, Ryder, let me go."

"You respond to me when I kiss you, Ashley, you can't deny that. Why are you fighting what you're feeling?"

"I'm not. Yes, I am," she said, wiggling out of his arms. "I'm not in the habit of kissing perfect strangers."

"Am I perfect?" he asked, grinning. Then he took a long, shuddering breath. "Whew! You really get to me, Ashley Hunt. What did you do? Whip up some magic potion from one of your plants?"

"Look, Cantrell, I mean Ryder, this is crazy. We don't even know each other."

"Your body knows who I am."

"That's disgusting!" she said, crossing her arms over her breasts.

"Your body? No way. It's soft and feminine, and

fits next to mine as if we were two peas in a pod. You are a very desirable woman."

"And you, no doubt, are used to getting whatever you want. I'll admit I responded to your kisses, but there aren't going to be any more."

"We'll see."

"I mean it, Cantrell!"

"Okay," he said calmly. "I think I'll buy a plant for Lucy."

"What?"

"It will be a peace offering. I fired her."

"You what?"

"She knows I didn't mean it, but it will be a nice gesture on my part, don't you think?"

"Cantrell, did you hear me say that you absolutely are not to kiss me again?"

"Sure. What kind of plant do you recommend?"

"I was right. You're despicable."

"Because I want to buy my sister a plant?"

"You just go around kissing whomever you please and it means nothing to you. I suppose the women you know just fall into your bed when you snap your fingers. Oh, forget it. I don't care what you do. I'll pick you out a nice African violet for Lucy."

"You're most kind," he said, suppressing a smile. Yep, Ashley Hunt was cute as a button, he thought. Oh, he was going to kiss her again, all right. No doubt about it. It was simply going to call for a little strategy. Why he was bothering with her, he didn't know. She was just different from the women he knew, like a breath of fresh air.

"Here," she said, shoving a pot at him. "Tell Lucy not to get the leaves wet when she waters it."

"How much do I owe you?"

"Five dollars."

Ryder set the plant on the desk and reached in

his pocket for the money. He peeled off a five-dollar bill and handed it to Ashley.

"Thank you," she said primly. "I appreciate your patronage."

"Is that all you appreciate about me?" he asked, flashing her a dazzling smile.

"Good-bye, Cantrell."

"I've been very patient with you, Miss Hunt. My name is Ryder, and from now on that is what you will call me."

"From now on? I intend never to see you again."

"You really are cute," he said, brushing a kiss across her lips before turning and picking up the plant. "See ya." He placed his fingers on the brim of his Stetson and strode out of the warehouse.

Ashley pressed her hand first to her lips and then to her forehead, to check her temperature. The man was driving her crazy! He was pushy and rude and . . . And when he kissed her she couldn't remember her own name! What was it about him, this Ryder Cantrell?

"Oh, who cares!" she said aloud. "I still say he's despicable. Well, not all the time but . . . Shut up, Ashley."

Outside, Ryder opened the door to the truck and placed the violet carefully on the seat.

"I've been waiting for you, Cantrell," he heard a man say behind him.

"Ah, hell," Ryder muttered, straightening as he turned to face Josh.

"Stay away from Ashley, Cantrell. I know your type. You're a user, a womanizer. Ashley isn't used to handling guys like you. Just don't come around her again."

"Go take a nap, kid," Ryder said, shaking his head in disgust. "You're way out of your league."

"Oh, yeah?" Josh replied, his face flushed with anger as he drew back his fist.

It was over before it began.

Ryder's left arm shot up to block Josh's punch, and an instant later Josh was flat on his back, on the ground, from the impact of Ryder's right fist.

"You broke my nose!" Josh yelled, struggling to sit up, then staring in horror at the blood dripping onto his shirt.

"It will give some character to your pretty face, ya know what I mean? Listen to me, Josh. Don't ever take me on again or you'll end up in a body cast. And as far as Ashley goes, I'll see her any time I damn well please."

Ryder slid behind the wheel of the truck and drove away, tires squealing, leaving Josh staggering to his feet. When Ryder stopped at the first intersection for a red light, he flexed the fingers on his right hand and grimaced.

"Dammit," he said, "the jerk messed up my hand. Ashley Hunt is not worth this!"

Josh meanwhile had hurried into the warehouse with his head tilted back and a handkerchief pressed to his nose.

"Ashley! I'm bleeding to death!"

"Josh, my heavens. What happened?"

"He tried to kill me!"

"Who did?"

"Cantrell."

Ashley squinted at Josh, who continued to moan.

"Who started it, Josh?" she asked.

"Don't you care that he broke my nose?"

"I asked you a question."

"I told him to stay away from you, Ashley, and he got real smart-mouthed about it, so I—"

"You did what? Josh, you have no right to inter-fere in my life."

"He's a womanizer, Ashley!"

"You don't even know him!"

"I know a womanizer when I see one, because—because I am one!"

"Huh?"

"Trust me. I could tell from the way he looked at you. Cantrell has a trained eye. Oh, yeah, he likes his women, all right. I don't want him anywhere near you."

"Joshua Smith, you are neither my father nor my brother. You have a lot of nerve!"

"I just went into battle for you, Ashley! Oh-h-h, my nose is swelling."

"Put an ice cube on it," she said, walking away. "Men! You are all ridiculous creatures."

"You're a cold woman, Ashley Hunt."

"Josh, put a cork in it!"

By the time Ryder returned to the office his right hand was throbbing and the arm ached all the way to his shoulder. Ryder Cantrell was not in a terrific mood.

"Here," he said, plunking the pot of violets in front of Lucy, "have a plant. You're supposed to water the leaves. No, wait. You're *not* supposed to water the leaves. Ah, hell, I can't remember. Give the thing a slug of beer."

"It's beautiful. Thank you, Ryder. Am I cele-brating something? Oh, I bet this means I'm not fired."

"Lucy, I'll buy you six plants if you'll do me a favor."

"Oh?"

"Wrap some ice cubes in a towel and bring them into my office with about a dozen aspirins."

"What have you done to yourself?"

"Just get the stuff!"

"Good grief. All right!"

When Lucy entered Ryder's office he was sitting behind his desk, scowling at his hand.

"Okay, where's your wound?" Lucy said. "Lord, your hand! What happened? Ryder, did you hit someone?"

"Me? Don't be silly. I'm a laid-back, easygoin' guy."

"Ha! What did that hand connect with?"

"The nose of a nerd."

"Let me see it."

"Oh, no, you don't. I've been the victim of your doctoring before and you've nearly killed me. Just give me the damn ice."

"What's all the hollerin' about?" Pappy asked, coming into the room.

"Ryder hurt his hand when he punched some guy out," Lucy explained.

"Serves him right, then," Pappy said.

"Thanks a whole helluva lot!" Ryder exclaimed. "I was simply defending myself against a muscle-bound kid who thinks he's been appointed the protector of women in Houston."

"I should have known," Lucy said. "There was a woman involved. Ho-ho, the light dawns. You bring me a plant and . . . Ashley Hunt. You went to see Ashley Hunt."

"I betcha that's the little filly who was out at the site yesterday," Pappy said.

"Give me that ice!" Ryder bellowed.

Pappy reached across the desk, picked up Ryder's hand in both of his, and pushed and pulled in one swift motion.

"Ow! Dammit to hell!" Ryder said.

"Was just unjammin' your knuckles," Pappy told him. "Put that ice on there now."

"You people drive me nuts," Ryder complained, applying the ice pack.

"I'm going to call Ashley," Lucy said.

"What in the hell for?" Ryder jumped to his feet.

"To find out how to take care of my violet. You were so busy being macho you forgot what she told you."

"Oh," he said, sinking back onto his chair.

"Take an aspirin," Lucy commanded, leaving the office.

Pappy chuckled under his breath and sat down in the chair opposite the desk. When he glanced up and saw Ryder's stormy expression, he burst into loud, cackling laughter.

"Do you have a problem?" Ryder asked through clenched teeth.

"Not me, boy. Nope, I'm fine. It's you that's all in a dither. How one pint-sized little girl can do in such a great big man, I'll never know."

"You don't know what you're talking about."

"We'll see. Comin' out to the ranch this weekend?"

"If I have time."

"Make time, boy. Do you good. Well," Pappy said, getting to his feet, "take care of that hand. How'd the other fella come out of this?"

"I broke his nose."

"Sounds fair. See ya later."

" 'Bye, Pappy," Ryder said absently. Why was his life suddenly so complicated? he wondered. He was a nice person. He worked hard, minded his own business, paid his taxes. And now Lucy was calling Ashley. Ashley was probably furious because he'd decked Mr. Body Beautiful. He'd warned that kid to back off, but had he listened? Hell, no. "Wonderful," Ryder muttered. "Now I've frozen my hand. I don't deserve this!"

Ashley answered the ringing telephone with a cheerful, "Plants-to-Go. May I help you?"

"Ashley, this is Lucy Cantrell. Do you remember me?"

"Yes, of course I do. How are you?"

"Fine. I have my lovely violet, but Ryder got your directions all mixed up. Am I supposed to water the leaves or not?"

"No, you mustn't get them wet. Lucy, I'm really very sorry about the names I called your brother yesterday. I was very upset and I had no idea who you were."

"Don't worry about it. I thoroughly enjoyed the whole thing. I . . . um . . . guess you had some excitement at your place a little while ago. Are you all right?"

"Oh, sure. I'm totally ignoring Josh and his moaning and groaning. The whole thing was his fault. Josh was way out of line and got his nose broken in the process. You'd think all those muscles would be worth more than that. Oh, well."

"Well, Josh Whoever has a hard nose, because Ryder jammed his knuckles."

"He's hurt?" Ashley yelled.

"No, no, he's just in a lousy mood. Grown men are such babies sometimes. Who is this Josh person anyway?"

"He's my friend. He does work for me here at the warehouse in exchange for room and board and a small salary. He and Ryder are not real fond of each other. The whole thing is so dumb."

"Interesting," Lucy said thoughtfully. "Ryder didn't go for the idea of Josh living there, right?"

"Ryder hollered his head off. I ask you, is it any of his business? No, it certainly is not! I managed to explain to Ryder that Josh was simply a good friend—not that I owed your brother an explanation, you understand—and then Josh goes crazy and says Ryder is a womanizer. Something to do with 'It takes one to know one,' and pow! Josh has a broken nose. As far as I'm concerned they can both take a hike."

"Absolutely."

"Are you sure Ryder's hand is all right?"

"Positive," Lucy said, a wide smile on her face. "He's very brave under the rigors of pain."

"Pain!"

"He'll be fine. Well, I must go. Thanks for the information about my violet. 'Bye, Ashley."

"What? Oh, yes, good-bye, Lucy."

Lucy hung up the receiver and rubbed her hands together.

"Oh, this is getting good," she said cheerfully. "I love it."

Ashley hung up her phone and frowned. Ryder had hurt his hand? she thought. Was he in pain? Oh, that Josh deserved his broken nose! But then again, Ryder *had* come across a little heavy, with his steely stare and rumbly voice, when he spoke to Josh. Oh, forget it. They were both idiots. But how much pain did jammed knuckles create?

"Ashley," Josh said, coming up behind her.

"Don't speak to me!" she ordered, flouncing away.

"Hell, I'm going out! Some women in this town appreciate me."

That night in bed, Ashley pushed aside the memories of the confrontation between Ryder and Josh and concentrated on the dilemma of losing her precious warehouse. She could buy a smaller place. Wrong. Without her large inventory of plants she could not possibly hope to service enough businesses to make a profit. Besides, she would not have the space to grow her new plants from cuttings, as she did now.

Renting a building was out of the question. She had discovered before buying the warehouse that no one was interested in renting to her, because of the changes she needed to make. Landlords worried about water damage, the wiring needed for her low-hanging fluorescent lights, everything.

"Oh, my," she murmured, sighing, "I don't have any answers. I just don't."

Ryder had a strange dream that night about plants growing over all the buildings he was constructing. The more he cut them away, the bigger they grew.

First thing the next morning an assessor arrived at the warehouse and a half hour later punched some figures into his pocket calculator. Ashley signed a paper and was told she would receive her check within the next few days. To her dismay, the amount quoted was even less than she had paid for the warehouse originally. Josh appeared at his bedroom door just as the assessor was leaving.

"Hi, Josh," she said absently as she stared at the sheet in her hand. "How's your nose?"

"Sore. What's that?"

"Look." She handed the paper to him.

"Hell, they ripped you off!"

"No, I apparently paid too much in the first place."

"What are you going to do, Ashley?"

"Well, I guess the first order of business is to notify everyone that I'm shutting down. My customers can decide whether they want to buy outright the plants that they have, and care for them, or have me pick them up."

"I have classes this morning, but I'll be back by

noon. I can go out in the van and get the ones people are returning."

"Thanks, Josh."

"Hang in there, sweetheart. We still have a roof over our heads."

"For a while."

"I've got to run. Will you be all right alone?"

"Yes, I'm okay. Josh, is your face dirty or are you getting black eyes?"

"Shiners, compliments of your macho boyfriend. It's not so bad. You wouldn't believe the sympathy I'm getting from the fair sex. I'm going to milk this for all it's worth."

"Oh, Josh." Ashley laughed. "You're so crazy."

"I still say you should stay away from Cantrell. He's—"

"Good-bye, Josh," she said, rolling her eyes.

Ryder spent the morning on the condominium job site. When he entered the office after lunch he found Lucy engaged in a one-sided conversation with her violet.

"You've flipped your switch, sister mine," he said. "Be sure to let me know when it starts answering back."

"You're supposed to talk to plants, Ryder. I wonder if I should give it a name."

"Spare me."

"How's your hand?"

"Stiff. Listen, do you realize how dull and drab this place is? It's cold, sterile. Blah."

"Blah?"

"Yeah, it needs some zing."

"Oh? Like plants, maybe?" Lucy batted her eyes at him.

"Now, why didn't I think of that?" he asked, smiling at her. "I swear, Lucy, you are just so smart."

"Oh, can it. Trot your little self over to Ashley's and buy some plants, which you intended to do in the first place."

"What frame of mind was she in when you called her yesterday?"

"Oh, not too bad," Lucy said, studying her fingernails. "She was simply ready to strangle you and Josh."

"Dammit, it wasn't my fault! The stupid kid just wouldn't back off."

"Tell it to the judge. Better yet, tell it to Ashley."

"Maybe I'll give her a few days to cool off."

"Suit yourself, but remember that Josh lives on the premises and can plead his case over and over."

"Good point. I think I'll just drop by there and get some plants for this place."

"Oh, Ryder? Gloria has called you three times today."

"Who?"

"Gloria? Tall, blond, big bazooms?"

"Oh, yeah, Gloria. Tell her I took a job in Siberia."

"She's going to be very unhappy with you."

"Hell, I don't care. I took her out a few times and now she thinks she owns me. Besides, she slithers."

"She what?"

"Slithers. You know, wiggles all over me. Drives me nuts."

"That's the price you pay for having a gorgeous body. You've never complained about attentive women before."

"Yeah, well, it gets old. I'll see you later," he said, leaving the office.

"Violet, dear," Lucy murmured, "the plot thickens."

When Ryder entered the warehouse he glanced

around for any sign of Josh. Satisfied that Ashley was alone, he pushed his Stetson back on his head and smiled at Ashley as she approached.

"Hello," she said quietly.

"Ashley, I want to explain about Josh and his nose."

"That's not necessary. How's your hand?"

"Fine. You're not angry about yesterday?"

"No, not really. I'm sure you both suffered enough for your foolishness. Anyway, I have other things on my mind."

"You seem down. Has something else happened?"

"The assessor was here. I'm getting less money than I put out for this place."

"Damn, that's rough. Is there a mortgage on the warehouse?"

"No, I paid cash. I received an inheritance from my grandmother."

"Can't you buy a smaller place?"

"It wouldn't work, Ryder. I need this much room to grow the plants. I've gone over every possibility in my mind and there's no solution. Josh is out picking up the plants from the people who don't want to tend to them."

"Then what?"

"I'll advertise and have a clearance sale. Then, that's it. I'm finished."

"Ashley, what are you going to do for a job?"

"I can always work for a nursery or a florist, I guess. It's just that owning my own business was my dream and . . . Well, I gave it my best shot."

"I'm really very sorry."

"I know, Ryder."

"That's twice you've called me Ryder instead of Cantrell."

"I did? I wasn't aware of it."

"I was. I like the way my name sounds when you say it. Will you have dinner with me tonight, Ashley?"

"Dinner?" Yes? No? What should she do? she wondered. Spend an entire evening in the company of Ryder Cantrell? Oh, dear heaven, that was dangerous. He did tricky little things to her reasoning power and caused her body to respond to him, as though he were pushing unseen buttons. No, absolutely not. She would be out of her mind to go out with this man!

"Ashley?"

She smiled. "Dinner would be lovely." Well, so much for her mind. She was a cuckoo. What a shame.

"I'll pick you up at seven."

"Fine."

" 'Bye," he said, kissing her quickly.

" 'Bye," she said, hardly above a whisper.

"Well?" Lucy asked when Ryder returned to the office.

"Well what?"

"Where are our spiffy new plants?"

"Our . . . Hell, I forgot."

"You went all the way over to Ashley's and forgot, *forgot*, to buy the plants?"

"Yeah. So what?"

"I can't believe this." Lucy dissolved in laughter.

"You have a strange sense of humor, Lucy," Ryder growled, pulling his Stetson forward on his head.

"Oh, my," she said, wiping tears of merriment off her cheeks.

"I'm going out to the condo site. Those guys are sane."

"Ryder, wait," Lucy said. "The nurse called from Dr. Metcalf's office. You're due for a checkup on your shoulder."

"I just had one."

"That was six months ago. I said I'd call back and schedule an appointment for you."

"I'm too busy right now."

"Ryder, please," she said quietly. "Don't play games with this. See the doctor, like you're supposed to."

Ryder looked down at his sister and saw the concern on her face, the flicker of pain in her eyes.

"I'd rather they'd call me directly," he said. "Every time I have to go in, you relive the whole thing. I wish so much that . . ."

"I know. So do I. Ryder, you don't still have the nightmares about it, do you?"

"No. I haven't had one in over a year. What about you, Lucy? When are you going to really start living again?"

"I have you, Pappy, my work, the ranch. That's enough for me."

"No, it isn't. You're a beautiful woman. You should have a husband, children."

"Not yet. I'm just not ready."

"It's been two years!"

"And sometimes it seems like only yesterday. I can still see it all so clearly."

"Don't. Let it go. It's all in the past, and you've got to start looking to the future."

"Like Ashley is?"

"What do you mean?"

"She's losing everything, and she'll have to start all over. Maybe I could learn something about courage from her."

"Maybe."

"And you, Ryder? What are you hoping to find in Ashley Hunt?"

"I don't know, Lucy. I really don't know."

Three

What did he hope to find in Ashley Hunt?

The question Lucy had asked seemed to hammer at Ryder as he showered and dressed for his dinner date. His answer to Lucy had been honest. He didn't know.

Ashley, with her braids and overalls, her natural freshness and unsophisticated demeanor, was a world apart from the women Ryder knew. He dated many and committed himself to none. The women had money, expected the finest, and took it all for granted.

Not so with Ashley Hunt. She had struggled to achieve her goal of owning her own business and was about to see it crushed beneath her feet. She evoked a protectiveness in Ryder that was different from that which he felt for Lucy. The emotions he had experienced when he had thought she was Josh's lover had been fierce, possessive. He knew he had been jealous as hell, and couldn't fathom why.

And as sure as he was standing there, the evening was not going to end with his taking Ashley to bed. No, she did not sleep around, he was sure of it. Ashley Hunt had class.

Actually, Ryder decided as he shrugged into his jacket, the whole thing was off-the-wall. Ashley was not his type and also would not satisfy his physical needs. Her life was a mess, and he didn't have any solutions for her. Nor did he have the time to get involved. Yet here he was, about to take her out, and looking forward to the evening ahead. Looking forward to it very, very much.

As Ryder reached for his watch, on top of the dresser, a sharp pain radiated through his left shoulder. He waited until it subsided, then wiped a line of perspiration off his brow.

"Damn," he muttered as he strode from the room.

Ashley bent over and brushed her heavy dark hair until it shone like an ebony cascade. She braided it into a single plait, then twisted it into a coil on the top of her head. Her dress was a lightweight cranberry wool that would be perfect for the cool spring night. Simply cut, the dress tapered in at her waist and fell in soft folds to mid-calf. She adorned the round neckline with a gold locket and stepped into three-inch black heels.

She felt pretty and feminine and carefree. Her buoyant mood was ridiculous, considering the precarious state of her life, but the evening ahead was hers. And Ryder's. Big, strong Ryder, who no doubt commanded the attention of women and the respect of men simply by walking into a room. Ryder, who was so comfortable and self-assured about his own masculinity that he had no qualms about being seen with a delicate violet in his large hands. His emerald eyes told many stories. They changed color with his moods: cold in anger, then warm and gentle, then smoky with desire.

Ryder Cantrell was like no man Ashley had ever known. She dated often, enjoyed the company of many men, and stood firm in her determination to bid good night at the door. She had resolved long ago that she would not give herself to a man unless she loved him. She was, she supposed, ridiculously old-fashioned, but she didn't care. It had not been difficult to keep sex out of her relationships, as there had been no one who stirred desire within her. Until now. Until Ryder.

When Ryder kissed her, she melted. She relished the feel of his lean body pressed to hers, and was sorry when the sensuous embraces ended. Her startling response to Ryder Cantrell was disconcerting, yet, somehow, didn't frighten her. It was as though she were discovering the mysteries of her inner self. She was definitely a woman.

Ashley left the small bedroom and walked across the echoing warehouse to her desk. She turned on the light there and a soft glow spread over the immediate area, leaving the remainder of the warehouse shrouded in darkness. A knock sounded at the locked door, and she hurried to answer it.

"Hello, Ryder." She smiled as she stepped back to allow him to enter.

He crushed his cigarette under his foot and walked forward, his gaze flickering over Ashley's slender figure in the pretty dress.

"Hello, Ashley," he said. "You look lovely."

"Thank you. So you do." He chuckled softly. He looked devastating, she thought. The faded jeans and shirt had been replaced by a perfectly tailored tan western-cut suit, a dark brown shirt, and a tie. He was just devastatingly handsome.

"Ready to go?" he asked.

"Certainly."

Outside, Ryder led Ashley to a low-slung silver sports car and opened the door for her. When he slid behind the wheel, Ashley glanced over at him, at his broad shoulders, his thick, silky hair, his large hands on the steering wheel. He was wearing a woodsy-scented after-shave that was fresh, male, and she averted her eyes as the tinglings began dancing up her spine.

Oh, man, Ryder thought, Ashley looked like an angel, all soft and feminine. What would her hair be like hanging free, spread out over his pillow as he—"How's things?" he asked, clearing his throat roughly as a shaft of heat shot across the lower regions of his body.

"Okay. How's Lucy's Saintpaulia?" Ashley asked as he edged into the traffic.

"Her what?"

"That, sir, is the official name for an African violet. I just thought I'd impress you with a little jargon."

"Her whatever is fine," he said, smiling. "She talks to it like a lunatic."

"Good for her. Now, that comes from a Nicotiana plant," she said as Ryder reached for a cigarette.

"Oh, yeah?" He laughed. "You're just full of great information. Do you have a degree in this stuff?"

"No, I took night classes at the university. I really didn't want a full agricultural degree, as my first love is growing plants in a nursery setting. I've always enjoyed working in the soil. I had a garden in our backyard, and new cuttings sprouting in my room everyplace we moved when I was young."

"Where is your family?"

"In Germany at the moment. My father is in the

Army. I have sixteen- and seventeen-year-old brothers. What about you?"

"Just Lucy and Pappy."

"Pappy? Your father?"

"No, we're not really related. It's a long story. Pappy is the little, gray-haired man who was out at the site."

"Oh, yes. I think he thought I was going to murder you."

"So did I for a minute there."

"Wasn't I terrific?" She laughed. "So ladylike and refined. Shame on me. I thought the bit about our starving baby was rather unique."

"My men sure enjoyed it."

"Ryder, is something wrong with your shoulder? Every time we stop at a red light you rub it. Josh didn't hurt more than your hand, did he?"

"No, and my hand is fine. My shoulder is just . . . a little tight. I didn't realize I was massaging it. It's really all right."

Ryder had made reservations at the Great Caruso Restaurant. Ashley loved the plush interior, with its many chandeliers hanging from the ceiling. Its velvet drapes and sweeping staircase reminded her of the inside of a castle. They were seated on a small balcony overlooking the main floor.

"I've decided to put some plants in my office," Ryder said after they'd ordered drinks. "You can pick them out and I'll buy them from your stock. Lucy can take care of them if you give her some instructions."

"Well, it'd be hard to pick out the plants without having seen your place. I need to know how much room you have, what type of lighting, that sort of thing. I really wasn't paying attention to all that the day I stormed in there. Ryder, why do you suddenly want plants?"

"Hey, it's not because you're in a bind and I'm try-

ing to help you reduce your inventory. I really . . . uh
. . . need some plants."

"Okay. Why don't I come over and look around
tomorrow?"

"Good."

"You know, now that I think about it, I should
have realized that Lucy is your sister. She has the
same coloring as you, hair, eyes. She's very pretty."

"Yeah, she is."

"She's not married?"

"No. She . . . Well, that's another long story. Are
you ready to order?"

"Yes, I'm really very hungry," Ashley said, picking
up the menu. Ryder was a private man, she thought.
He was charming, put her at ease, but he was holding
a portion of himself back, not really sharing much
about himself. She had seen him reach again for his
shoulder, then pull his hand away as if not wishing to
draw attention to it. When he spoke of Pappy and
Lucy, his voice had a gentle quality. Were there no
others he allowed to enter into his world, his space?
she wondered. Had a woman ever known all of Ryder
Cantrell?

They ordered steak and lobster, baked potatoes
with mounds of sour cream, and fresh asparagus
swimming in butter. Ryder asked Ashley endless
questions about her childhood, and what it had been
like growing up in a military family. She told him
about the various countries she had lived in, and
then explained that after graduating from high
school she had moved to Houston to be near her ail-
ing grandmother. She had worked in a large nursery
and saved her money, dreaming of someday owning
her own business. Her voice became hushed as she
spoke of the death of her grandmother a year earlier,
but she brightened an instant later as she recounted

he excitement of using her inheritance to purchase
he warehouse and making Plants-to-Go a reality.

"You know," she said as they sipped their coffee,
'all we've done is talk about me. I still don't know very
nuch about you."

"Well," he replied, lighting a cigarette, "there's
iot much to tell. I'm in construction and own a small
·anch just outside of town. Lucy and Pappy live out
here, but I keep an apartment in the city, because I
·an't get away that often. My foreman runs the ranch,
'appy does whatever strikes his fancy, and Lucy
vorks for me."

"When you haven't fired her."

"True."

"The three of you are very close."

"Yes, we are. We're . . . all we have."

"You've never been married?"

"No, I was busy getting Cantrell Construction on
·ts feet, then later the ranch. That land is important
·o me, because I wanted to be sure that Pappy would
iave somewhere he would be contented as he grew
·lder. Then, two years ago . . . Well, time just has a
vay of passing. I just haven't settled down yet."

Two years ago what? Ashley wondered. He had
·tarted to tell her something, then stopped. Why?
Vhy did he do that?

"I'm glad you came out with me tonight, Ashley,"
Ryder said, covering her hand with his on the top of
he table. "I've really enjoyed talking to you, getting to
:now you better. I think you're very courageous, the
vay you're accepting everything that's happened
vith your warehouse, the business, your dream."

"I'm not brave, just realistic. I have no choice but
·o keep moving forward. I'm bitterly disappointed
·bout the way things turned out, but there's nothing
  can do about it. I'm sure not everything in your life
vent the way you hoped."

"No," Ryder said, his jaw tightening slightly, "i certainly didn't."

Their eyes met in a long, steady gaze, and Ashley was aware of the heat emanating from Ryder's hand. The warmth seemed to travel up her arm and across her breasts, causing her heart to beat a sharp tattoo. She felt almost light-headed. She tried desperately to read the expression in his green eyes, to gain some clue about what he was thinking. She saw a gentleness there, a warm glow, and something else she couldn't quite decipher.

"Do you ever wear your hair down?" he asked suddenly.

"Not often. It gets in my way when I'm working with the plants. The sensible thing would be to cut it, I suppose."

"No, don't. It must look like a raven waterfall when it's hanging down your back. Don't cut your hair, Ashley."

"All right," she said breathlessly. Good heavens, she thought. Ryder was weaving a web around her sense of reasoning. If he kept this up she was liable to agree to anything! "Excuse me, I'm going to the powder room."

Ryder stood as Ashley left the table, then sank back into his chair and absently rubbed his shoulder which was increasingly painful.

Something strange had come over him as he was talking to Ashley, he thought, a frown creasing his brow. He had wanted to tell her everything about Pappy, about himself, about what had taken place two years ago. He had actually had to struggle to push it all away and not pour out his soul to her. Why? Why her? Oh, what luxury it would be to speak of the past and perhaps free himself of the haunting memories. What ecstasy not to have to be so big and strong and tough, and for a brief time share his inner burdens.

with her. No, he hadn't done it and wouldn't allow himself to in the future. But the fact remained that in that fleeting moment, he had wanted to.

"The powder room is decorated so beautifully," Ashley said as she sat back down. "I wish you could go in there and see it. Oh, what a dumb thing to say."

Ryder laughed in delight, and signaled the waiter for the check.

"Ashley," Ryder said, "it's not terribly late, and I really don't want to take you home yet. Would you come back to my apartment for a nightcap?"

"Well . . ."

"You don't have a living room, I doubt seriously if you want to entertain me in your bedroom, and I could really do without bumping into Josh in the kitchen. So? My place?"

"You plead a good case, counselor," she said, smiling. "All right, your place." Yes, she was definitely out of her mind, she thought. Where was her common sense? It had drowned, like everything else, in the deep pools of Ryder Cantrell's emerald green eyes.

The Texas sky was like an umbrella of stars as Ryder maneuvered his sleek sports car through the traffic with ease. Ashley recognized the area they entered as being that of the affluent, the money men of Houston. That Ryder lived there came as no surprise to her, nor did it intimidate her in any way. Ryder worked hard for his money, as she did. The fact that he paid more taxes than she held little significance.

No, she thought, it wasn't wealth that gave him his aura of power, it was the man himself. The square set to his shoulders, the eyes that missed no detail, the lazy rolling gait that did not mask the underlying strength, made Ryder a man to be reckoned with.

Ashley shivered slightly as she realized that she,

too, was falling prey to Ryder's magnetism. His kiss and touch, his heated gazes, were unsettling her equilibrium, throwing her off-balance. She was now on her way to this man's apartment, and for the life of her she couldn't open her mouth and tell him to take her home. And, to top it off, she was becoming nervous, getting a roaring case of the jitters.

"Relax," Ryder said quietly. "Would you prefer that I take you home?"

"No, of course not. I . . . No."

"What's wrong, Ashley?"

"Wrong? Nothing is wrong. My goodness, everything is just fine."

"Right. That's why you're talking a hundred miles an hour."

"I am?"

He chuckled. "You are."

He pulled into an underground garage and parked in a space marked "Cantrell." As he helped her out of the car, her glance fell on similar signs marking the spaces on either side, where pickup trucks were parked. They rode up in the elevator in silence and emerged in a carpeted hallway. Ryder unlocked a door, pushed it open, and stepped back for her to enter.

"Make yourself at home," he said, flicking on the lights. "I just want to get rid of this tie."

Ashley nodded, and watched as Ryder disappeared into the bedroom. She had to get a grip on herself, she thought as she sank onto the sofa. Granted, she knew she wasn't as sophisticated as the women Ryder was probably used to, but this was ridiculous! She'd been in men's apartments before. But not Ryder Cantrell's! So, big deal. He was just a man. Who was she kidding? He was the person who turned her into Silly Putty just by gazing at her with those damnable green eyes. Okay, she was calm now.

She'd have a drink and discuss the state of the economy. Oh, help!

Ryder shrugged out of his jacket and pulled his tie loose, tossing both onto the bed. He walked into the bathroom and quickly swallowed two aspirins before massaging his aching shoulder. The damn thing was going crazy, he thought. He didn't need it, not now. He'd have to see Metcalf and find out what was going on. Well, he'd ignore it tonight, because Ashley was waiting for him in the living room. She'd tensed up, was obviously nervous about being in his apartment. Well, he could handle that. They'd have a quick drink and he'd take her home, so she'd see she had nothing to worry about. He wouldn't do *anything* that would frighten Ashley Hunt!

But why was he going to all this trouble? he asked himself. Hell, at this point in an evening there should have been a woman in his bed. Why all this fuss and bother over a wide-eyed girl who didn't know how to play the game? He wasn't going to get anything out of this except a cold shower and a strung-out libido, because, oh, yes, he did desire Ashley. He had mental pictures of that beautiful hair loose and spread out on his pillow. Her breasts were small and firm, and would fit into the palms of his hands.

"Stow it, Cantrell," he muttered as he felt an ache in his loins.

When Ryder entered the living room Ashley was standing at the window, looking out over the skyline of Houston. He walked up behind her and placed his hands gently on her shoulders, resisting the urge to pull her against him, to feel the soft curves of her body pressed to the hardness of his own. He could smell her lemony shampoo and pictured himself taking the pins from her hair and . . .

"You have a lovely view," Ashley said.

"Yeah, it's nice. Would you like a drink?"

"Yes, please," she answered, turning to face him.

Ryder dropped his arms to his sides and took a step backward as he gazed down at her. She smiled slightly and he walked to the bar to pour their drinks. Ashley sat on the sofa and accepted her snifter, feeling the cushions give under Ryder's weight as he sat down only a few inches away from her. She took a deep swallow of the amber liquid and coughed as it burned her throat.

"Easy, there," he suggested, taking her glass and setting it on the coffee table. "That's brandy. You're supposed to sip it."

"I think I just dissolved my tonsils."

Ryder chuckled and placed his glass next to hers.

"Ashley," he said quietly, "you have no reason to be afraid of me. I think your Josh did a number on you about what kind of man I am. I don't force myself on women."

"Why would you have to?" she asked miserably. "You probably carry a big stick to beat them off."

Ryder laughed and shook his head, then circled Ashley's shoulders with one arm and pulled her close. She rested her head on his shoulder, feeling the rich silk of his shirt beneath her cheek, filling her senses with his special aroma. They sat quietly for several minutes, then Ryder shifted slightly and tilted her chin up with one finger.

The kiss was so gentle, so soft, that Ashley felt suddenly close to tears. Ryder was moving slowly, tentatively, so as not to frighten her, and she was overwhelmed by his sensitivity. As his tongue sought entry to her mouth, she complied, leaning slightly toward him. His arms moved the moment that hers did, his to wrap around her back, hers to entwine about his neck. The kiss intensified, became more urgent, as tongues met and dueled. Ryder's hand slid up to cup her breasts, his thumbs trailing over her already taut nipples.

Ashley's trepidation was swept away by the desire that surged within her. Like sand being blown from the palm of a hand, her fears vanished as she returned his kiss in total abandonment. She could feel the heat coursing through her body as her passion heightened, and she welcomed its arrival. She felt alive as never before as the new and mysterious sensations exploded within her.

Ryder lifted his head slightly to draw a ragged breath, then claimed her mouth again, plunging his tongue deep into the inner darkness. She moaned softly as his hands continued the tantalizing exploration of her breasts, which were throbbing beneath his maddening touch. There was no time or space, or reality or reason, as Ashley sank her fingers into his thick hair to press his mouth harder onto hers.

"Ashley." Ryder gasped. "I— Damn." He pulled her arms free and took a deep breath.

"Ryder?" she whispered, suddenly confused, uncertain.

He didn't speak for a minute as he strove for control, his gaze fastened on the snifters on the coffee table. He ran his hand down his face and looked at the ceiling for a moment, then turned to her.

"I'm sorry," he said. "I shouldn't have done that. I gave you a big spiel about how safe you are with me and then I . . . I'm really very sorry."

"I knew what I was doing, Ryder," she said softly.

"Did you? I'm not so sure of that. Ashley, you remind me of a flower that is just opening its petals to discover a world it's never known. I desire you. I want to make love to you, but I have to ask you this: Have you ever been with a man?"

"Oh, wonderful," she said, crossing her arms over her breasts. "Is this where I'm interviewed to see if I have enough experience for you? Lord, I can't believe this!"

"Dammit, answer the question!"

"No, I won't, because it's none of your business, Ryder Cantrell. I'm not quizzing you about how many lovers you've had. You've probably lost count anyway. You really have a lot of nerve!"

"I'm trying to protect you from—"

"From whom? You? Myself? Just when were you appointed my keeper?"

"You are really pushing me, lady," he said, getting to his feet.

"What are you going to do? Break my nose?"

"No." His eyes flashed with anger. "I was thinking more in terms of kissing you until you can't breathe or even think. Then I'd remove your clothes very slowly and caress every inch of that delectable body of yours. I'd make you want me so badly you'd be begging me to come to you and make love to you until dawn."

"Oh, dear me," Ashley whispered, pressing her hands to her cheeks.

"See? You're getting in over your head." He reached for a pack of cigarettes on the coffee table, shook one loose, and lit it.

"I am perfectly capable of taking care of myself."

"Oh? Well, then I can assume that you're on some sort of birth control."

"Birth control?" she repeated in a small voice.

"Oh, Lord!" he said, crushing the cigarette in the ashtray. "What am I going to do with you?"

"Do?"

"You are driving me nuts!" he roared.

"Then take me home to my plants and forget you ever met me!" she yelled, jumping to her feet.

"Believe me, I wish I could. I really do, but there's

no way in hell I can walk away from you now. I don't know what it is about you, but—"

"Ryder," she interrupted him, "you're holding your shoulder again. There's really something wrong with it, isn't there?"

"It's all right," he said gruffly.

"Why won't you tell me about it? You don't let me get close to you, Ryder. You start to say things and then you stop as if you don't trust me enough to really share yourself."

"It's not that I don't trust you, Ashley. I think it's because I trust you too much."

"I don't understand."

"You are so special, so different from any woman I have ever known. You scare the hell out of me because I'm feeling things that are foreign to me. I feel protective, possessive, toward you and I want to talk to you for twenty-four hours straight and tell you everything that's happened to me from the day I was born. I desire you more than I ever have any woman before, and I have the depressing thought that I'm not going to seduce you, even though I'm aching with wanting you. You are turning my mind into scrambled eggs, and I think you're the classiest lady I've had the pleasure of meeting."

"Thank you," she said, smiling at him warmly. "No one has ever said I was classy."

"Well, you are," he assured her, walking over and pulling her into his arms. "I really wish I knew what I was going to do about you."

"You make me sound like a disease," she joked, resting her head on his chest.

"Close."

"Well, thanks a bunch."

"You know what it's like when something sneaks into your system and you can't shake it off? From the minute you came storming onto my job site you've been taking up a lot of my mental space. You are definitely getting to me, Ashley Hunt. Of course, I could be taking a lot for granted here."

"Like what?"

"For all I know you could be about to tell me to get out of your life and leave you alone."

"I don't want to do that, Ryder."

"That's good, because I doubt if I'd give up so easily. You'd end up hiring Josh as your bodyguard."

"A lot of protection he'd be," she said, laughing. "His overabundance of muscles is useless."

"He's got the physique, but not the street sense. His reflexes are slow. Where I grew up you learned very quickly to— Never mind. Come on, I'll take you home."

"Where did you grow up, Ryder?"

"Here, there, and everywhere. Listen, why don't you come by the office just before noon tomorrow to check it out for my plants, and then I'll take you and Lucy to lunch?"

"That sounds like fun. And, Ryder? If you ever decide to talk, I'll listen. Really listen."

"I know that, Ashley. It's just very difficult for me to open up about . . . We'll see what happens, okay? Let's just take this slow and easy, one day at a time."

"I think that sounds just fine."

"Yes, ma'am," he said, cupping her face in his large hands. "You are a very classy lady."

Ryder kissed her softly on the lips, then on her cheeks, the end of her nose, her forehead. Smiling at her warmly, he circled her shoulders with his arm and they left the apartment.

Much later Ashley lay in bed, staring up into the darkness. She felt weary, drained. The evening with Ryder had encompassed so many emotions, and she felt as though she had journeyed to a faraway place and returned. Ryder Cantrell was a very complicated man. He held a tight rein on his thoughts and emotions, yet expressed a desire to share them with her. At the same time he held back, refusing to trust her completely, although he demanded complete honesty from her. He wasn't sure he cared for the feelings she evoked in him, but was adamant about continuing to see her. He wanted her physically, yet had called a halt as their ardor grew. He was confusing and exhausting and . . .

"Wonderful," she said aloud, flopping over onto her stomach. "I like you, Ryder Cantrell. I like you very, very much."

The next morning Ashley put together ads for the newspapers, announcing a clearance sale and giving directions to the warehouse. She had decided to hold the sale on Saturday, so Josh would be available in case there was a huge turnout.

"I hope people come," she said to Josh.

"Sure, they will," he said. "Your prices are so low you're practically giving the stuff away. I heard you come in late last night. Big date?"

"I had a lovely time."

"With who?"

"None of your business."

"Cantrell. You just won't listen to me, will you?"

"Don't start again, Josh. I've heard your bit about Ryder's being a womanizer. You're standing in judgment on someone you don't even know."

"His type I know. Where did he take you?"

"Out to dinner."

"And?"

"For a drink. Josh, go to class."

"Where for a drink?"

"His apartment."

"Cripe! You are such a dunce, Ashley!"

"Nothing happened! Why am I having this conversation with you?"

"Ashley, the man is a hustler! He probably has to swat women away like flies. He's out of your league, and you're going to end up hurt. The Cantrells of this world sleep with women, but they sure as hell don't marry them. He's got a mean streak, too. He broke my nose."

She shrugged. "He says your reflexes are slow."

"I'll kill him!"

"Josh, shut up. You said yourself you grew up with oodles of money and the only reason you're so busted now is because your family booted you out when you refused to become an Episcopalian priest, as they'd planned from the day you were born. All Ryder meant was that, while you have a great physique, you don't have that sense of survival that comes from being on the streets."

"He said I had a great physique?" Josh grinned.

"Oh, go away."

"Was he saying he grew up on the streets? But the guy is loaded with money. He does, however, have a very fast right hook. So what's the scoop? Was he a street fighter?"

"I don't know. He doesn't talk much about himself."

"Maybe he's an ex-con. Now, those guys know how to take care of themselves. I'll bet he's—"

"Joshua!"

"Okay, okay, I'm leaving. Are you going to see Cantrell again?"

"Yes."

"When?"

"Good-bye, Mr. Smith."

Ashley frowned as she watched Josh leave the warehouse. She really knew so little about Ryder, she thought. Had he grown up defending himself on the streets? If so, where had all his money come from? Would Ryder lower the walls he'd constructed and share himself with her? Why did it matter so much to her whether he did?

"And he says that *I'm* getting to *him*?" Ashley said to a Boston fern. "*He's* consuming my brain! And my body is in even worse shape. Oh, good grief."

Dressed in a white skirt and pale pink blouse, her hair twisted into a coil on top of her head, she arrived at Ryder's office at eleven-thirty.

"Hi, Ashley," Lucy said.

"Hello, Lucy."

"I hear my big brother is taking us to lunch. That lucky devil. He'll have a ravishing beauty on each arm. Order the most expensive thing on the menu. He can afford it."

"Well, first I have to decide what plants to put in here. Do you have any favorite kinds?"

"I don't know one from the other except for Violet, here."

"Who watches the office when you go out?"

"I put on the phone answering machine. You would not believe what some people say. It's really obscene." Lucy laughed merrily.

"Lucy, I want to ask you something, but I realize it's none of my business. Please feel free not to answer if you'd rather, but I'm worried about it, that's all."

"What is it, Ashley?"

"Is there . . . Is there something wrong with Ryder's left shoulder? He says there isn't, but—Lucy? My gosh, you're white as a ghost. I didn't mean to upset you. I'm so sorry."

"No, no, it's not your fault." Lucy took a shaky breath. "I'm just so unstable about everything connected with . . . You've seen Ryder holding his shoulder?"

"Yes, I have. He just shrugged it off, but I think he was in a lot of pain."

"Yes, I've seen it too," Lucy said quietly. "He tries to hide it when I'm around, because the whole thing is a living nightmare for me. I want desperately to put it away once and for all, but I don't seem capable of doing it."

"I don't understand."

"You'd think that after two years I'd be in better shape, but I fall apart every time I think about it. That's why Ryder never tells me when his shoulder is bothering him. I had the feeling it was in bad shape this time, but I wasn't positive. From what you've said, I was right. I—"

"Lucy . . ." Ryder said, striding toward them down the hall. "Hello, Ashley Hunt." He smiled at her.

"Hello, Ryder." Her heart started racing at the sight of him.

"Lucy, get me a reservation on a plane to Austin, preferably within the next hour or so. I've got problems on the job up there."

"But you can't go to—"

"I'll buy you both lunch as soon as I get back, I promise. Get on the phone."

"Ryder," Lucy said, "I made an appointment for you to see Dr. Metcalf about your shoulder this afternoon."

Ryder looked quickly at Ashley before redirecting his attention to his sister.

"Cancel it," he said, his jaw tight. "Don't make a big deal out of it, just reschedule it for some other time."

"No! You've got to see Dr.—"

"That's enough, Lucy. Make me that plane reservation. I'm going home to pack, and I'll phone you from the apartment to find out what time my flight is."

"Ryder?" Ashley said.

"I'll see you soon," he said, walking over to her. "Don't worry about any of this. Lucy's just a little strung out. The two of you go on out to lunch."

"But—"

" 'Bye," he said, kissing her quickly. "Call the airlines, Lucy," he yelled as he left the office.

"Damn you, Ryder Cantrell!" Lucy said.

"Dear heaven, what is going on here?" Ashley whispered.

Four

Ashley spun around as she heard a thud, and saw that Lucy had tossed the heavy telephone book onto the desk and was flipping through it with a vengeance. A moment later, Lucy snatched the telephone receiver and punched out the number of the airline. Having made Ryder's plane reservation, Lucy slammed the receiver back into place and promptly burst into tears.

"Oh, Lucy," Ashley said, hurrying to her side, "don't cry."

"I'm sorry." She sniffled. "I'm a wreck, a basket case, an emotional cripple."

"No, no. Calm down, now. Let's go out for a quiet lunch and—"

"I have to wait for Mr. Idiot to call, so I can tell him when to catch his stupid plane."

"Look, you go wash your face and I'll answer the phone. Okay?"

"Well, all right. I don't want to speak to Ryder Cantrell anyway." Lucy stomped down the hall.

Ashley settled onto Lucy's chair and folded her hands primly on the top of the desk. Wonderful, she thought. Now she was playing secretary for a construction company she knew absolutely nothing about. Lucy was terribly upset about Ryder's canceling his doctor's appointment for his shoulder. But it was more than that. Something else was causing his sister to be close to hysteria. Ryder himself had been reluctant to draw any attention to the pain he was obviously experiencing. What was wrong with him? she wondered, suddenly deeply concerned. It wasn't serious, was it? She couldn't bear it if—

"Good Lord." The telephone rang, jarring her out of her reverie, and she spoke cautiously into the receiver. "Cantrell Construction."

"Who?"

"Cantrell Construction. May I help you?"

"Ashley?"

"Ryder?"

"Yeah. Where's Lucy?"

"She went to the ladies' room. Ryder, she's terribly upset."

"I know," he said, sounding suddenly weary. "I wish that hadn't happened. Well, it's done. Did she make my reservation?"

Ashley quickly read off the information scribbled on a piece of paper.

"Okay, thanks. Ashley, I really don't want to go to Austin right now, and it's not just because of Lucy. When I came down that hall and saw you standing there I . . . I'll be thinking about you while I'm gone and I'll call you the minute I get back."

"All right."

"I dreamed about you last night," he said, his

voice low, seeming to caress her like a velvet glove. "You kept me company until dawn."

"Oh," she said. Oh? That was all she could say? she thought. Just oh?

"Miss me a little, okay?"

"Well, sure."

"Good. Ashley, I hate to ask you to take this on, but would you try to get Lucy to go out to lunch with you? Push a bit, get her to talk about this thing that's ripping her up. She needs a friend."

"Of course I will. Ryder, your shoulder. What is—"

"I'll see the doc as soon as I get back. Don't worry about it."

"But—"

"I've got to go. Take care of yourself, and I'll see you soon. 'Bye."

"Good-bye, Ryder," she said, and slowly replaced the receiver.

Ashley rested her elbows on the desk and cupped her chin in her hands. The image of Ryder danced before her eyes. She heard his laughter, could vividly recall his special aroma. Her body tingled with the memory of his kiss, his touch, his—

"Ashley?" Lucy asked.

"What?" Ashley jumped in surprise.

"Did Ryder call?"

"Yes. I gave him the information about his flight. Come on, let's go out to lunch."

"I wouldn't be very good company. I do apologize for my performance."

"Lucy, I'm caught in the middle here. Ryder asked me to see if I could get you to talk about what's bothering you. The thing is, I want to do that, to be your friend, but not as a favor to Ryder. I want to do it for myself. Do you understand?"

"Yes, and I appreciate it. You'd be taking on an

awful lot, though. My world fell apart, and I've never been able to put it back together. I wish I were as strong as you are."

"Me? Oh, Lucy, I'm not that tough. I just don't have any choice but to plow ahead."

"Well, I admire you for your fortitude. Maybe— maybe if I talked it out I could . . . I don't know."

"Turn on your obscene machine and we'll go find a quiet restaurant."

"All right."

Neither spoke during the short walk to the restaurant. They were seated in a dimly lit, secluded corner, and each ordered a salad.

Ashley wanted to help Lucy, to be her friend, but a part of her was held in an icy grip of fear that Lucy would tell her that something was seriously wrong with Ryder's shoulder. She would stay calm, she told herself firmly, no matter what Lucy said. If she fell apart, Lucy no doubt would, too, and the restaurant owner would have two hysterical women on his hands.

"I just realized," Lucy remarked, "that Ryder kissed you before he left the office."

"Well, it was just a peck," Ashley said, grateful the warm flush on her cheeks was not visible, thanks to the subdued lighting.

"Yes, but he did it so naturally, so automatically. That really isn't like him. Interesting. Of course, he's been acting rather strangely ever since he met you. You're very different from the . . . Well, never mind."

"From the other women in his life?" Ashley asked.

"The flash-and-dash gals. They swarm over him like bees looking for nectar, and they make me sick. I'm so glad Ryder found you, Ashley."

"Lucy, please don't read more into this than there is. I'm really not his type."

"We'll see. I . . . uh . . . guess I can't postpone this any longer. I have the feeling that if I don't talk to you right now I'll never get the courage to do it again. Oh, here's our lunch."

Their plates were set before them, and the waiter moved away. Ashley took a bite of her crab salad, but hardly tasted it, as she waited for Lucy to continue speaking.

"There was a man," Lucy said quietly, "named Jimmy Larson, who was one of Ryder's top construction workers, a foreman. He and Ryder became close friends, and Ryder began to bring Jimmy out to the ranch. Well, before very long Jimmy and I fell in love. I had never been so happy as I was the day he asked me to marry him."

"Was Ryder pleased?"

"Oh, yes. He and Jimmy were like brothers, and Pappy went around grinning from ear to ear. We were going to be married as soon as the job Jimmy was in charge of was completed, which was about a month away. Then I found out I was pregnant. Jimmy was ecstatic, and so was I."

"But what about Ryder? What did he do?"

She shrugged. "Nothing. He said he'd be a terrific uncle and planned to spoil the baby rotten. He offered to take over the job for Jimmy so we could get married right away and go on a honeymoon. Ryder was to spend a few days on the site so Jimmy could bring him up-to-date on where everything stood. They had been working together for two days when I decided to drive out to the site and see if Jimmy could have lunch with me. I— Oh, God, Ashley, I can't do this."

"What happened when you got there, Lucy?" Ashley said gently. "Tell me."

"Jimmy and Ryder were—were on a scaffold seventy feet above the ground that was suspended from an overhead beam by four heavy metal cables. I was standing below with Pappy, watching them, when . . ."

Ashley waited as Lucy strove for control. Lucy was staring off into space as if she were completely reliving the scene.

"One of the cables broke," Lucy went on. "Jimmy started to fall, and Ryder grabbed his wrist. Jimmy's weight caused Ryder to slip, and he hung on to the scaffold with his right arm and to Jimmy with his left. Everyone was yelling and scrambling to get up there to them, but it was as though they were moving in slow motion."

"And then?"

"Ashley, oh, Ashley, the other cable broke on the same end as the first one. It whipped around and caught Ryder in the left shoulder. It just tore into him with as much force as a bullet, and . . . and he lost his grip on Jimmy's wrist."

"Dear God," Ashley whispered.

"Jimmy fell all the way to . . . My beloved died."

"Oh, Lucy," Ashley said, taking her hand, "I'm so very sorry."

"Ryder held on with his right arm. To this day no one knows how he did it, considering the pain he was in. I really don't remember much after that. I woke up in the hospital, Jimmy was dead, and Ryder was in surgery for his shoulder. A few weeks later, I had a miscarriage. I wanted to die, I really did. I just wanted to die. It was Pappy who sat with me, held me when I cried and screamed at everyone. I blamed myself because if I hadn't gotten pregnant, Ryder wouldn't have been stepping in, they wouldn't have been on the scaffold together, and . . . I don't know, nothing made sense."

"And Ryder?"

"He was so badly hurt. He was in surgery for hours to repair the damage to his shoulder, and it was months before he had full use of his arm again. He had nightmares about the accident, about letting go of Jimmy. We were out at the ranch, and I'd hear Pappy go to Ryder in the night to wake him up, because Ryder would be calling to Jimmy."

"Lucy," Ashley said, hastily brushing the tears from her cheeks, "what is going on with Ryder's shoulder now?"

"He has to have a checkup every six months. The last time, the doctor said that some of the scar tissue was moving closer to the nerve endings and that Ryder should pay attention to any increase in pain. And now it's happening. There's something drastically wrong, and that stubborn fool went off to Austin instead of going to the doctor. Oh, Lord, now I've upset you. I know you care for Ryder. I'm so selfish. I sit here pouring out my tale of woe without thinking of how it would affect you."

"I'm glad you told me. I know you loved Jimmy, Lucy, but he wouldn't want you to go on grieving for him. He'd want you to be happy, live a full life."

"That's what Ryder and Pappy say. I'm going to try harder, I really am. Ashley, Ryder will be all right. I just overreact to anything that has to do with the accident."

"I knew he was in pain, I just knew it. What a dumb-dumb! He should have stayed here and gone to the doctor."

Lucy laughed. "You're terrific. Look at me! I'm actually smiling. Thank you, Ashley, so very much."

"Have I got a guy for you! Curly black hair, muscles, economy-sized ego."

"Josh!"

"Right. He's a little young, but maybe that means he's trainable."

"I'll pass. How gorgeous can he be? He has a broken nose!"

The remainder of the meal passed pleasantly as the two women chatted about various topics. They strolled leisurely back to the office building, and Ashley promised to pick out some plants that would look splendid in the reception area of Cantrell Construction.

Back at the warehouse, Ashley changed into jeans and a cotton blouse and sank onto the edge of the bed. She felt a knot tighten in her stomach as she reconsidered the story Lucy had told of Jimmy and Ryder. Through force of will and by brute strength Ryder had held on to the scaffold until help came. So many lives had been changed that day, and now Ashley, too, was feeling its ramifications. The ordeal was not yet over for Ryder. And because he was in pain, so was Ashley.

She gathered together a nice selection of plants for Ryder's office and placed them by the front door to load into the van the next morning. Josh arrived at dinner time, complaining about a difficult exam he was facing, and the pair spent the evening in the kitchen, with Ashley quizzing him on the complicated material.

Ashley's dreams that night were plagued by distorted figures falling through dark holes in space, by hands reaching for unseen objects, by Ryder Cantrell opening his mouth to speak, but making no sound.

Pappy was at Cantrell Construction the next morning when Ashley arrived, and he volunteered to help tote the plants up from the van.

"Lucy told me you two had a good talk yesterday," Pappy said as they unloaded the van.

"Yes, we did. It must have been difficult for you, too, to witness the accident, Mr. . . . ."

"Call me Pappy. Yeah, it was a mighty bleak day. After Jimmy fell, I was yellin' at Ryder to hang on, even though I knew he couldn't hear me. Lord only knows where he got the strength."

"What do you think is going to happen about his shoulder now, Pappy?"

"I don't know. We'll have to wait for the doc to take a look at it. Ryder's been workin' too hard, pushin' himself, and he was warned about doin' that. I'm thinkin' maybe he'll have other things on his mind from now on, though."

"Like what?"

Pappy smiled. "Oh, a little brown-eyed filly with pigtails."

"Oh, dear me," Ashley said, blushing crimson.

"You know, missy, it's going to take a lot of patience to deal with that boy, but he's worth every minute. He's the finest man I know. But then, I think you've figured out that he's a cut above the rest."

"He's very special," she said quietly.

"Remember, now, patience."

"I'll remember, Pappy."

Lucy raved about the plants, and while she didn't mention their conversation of the previous day, she hugged Ashley tightly.

"I'd better get back to the warehouse," Ashley said. "My big sale starts tomorrow, and I want to make sure everything is properly tagged. Has . . . uh . . . Ryder called from Austin?"

"No." Lucy immediately frowned. "When he goes on a site to troubleshoot, he hardly takes time to eat or sleep."

"But his shoulder!"

"Me and my big mouth," Lucy said. "I'm sorry, Ashley. I didn't mean to upset you. All we can do is wait for him to get home, and then drag him bodily to the doctor."

"What a dimwit he is!" Ashley stomped out of the office.

"Patience, missy," Pappy called after her. "Have lots of patience."

Josh was waiting for Ashley when she returned to the warehouse, and she knew within moments of saying hello that he was nervous about something.

"Okay, Josh, what's up?" she asked.

"Well, I . . . Well, you see . . ."

"Josh!"

"Yes! Okay! There's this girl named Debbie Mary Sue, who—"

"Debbie Mary Sue?"

"Yeah, she's a southern belle. Anyway, we've been going out a lot and getting along fine, and she has this big apartment and . . ."

"You're moving in with her."

"You really don't need me anymore, Ashley. There just won't be anything for me to do once the sale is over. I figured I'd better get a roof over my head while I had a chance."

"That's a crummy reason to move in with someone. Ever heard of love? Commitment?"

"Please, I'm fragile. Those words blow my mind. Debbie Mary Sue is a good kid. We'll have a fun time."

"I understand, Josh. I'll miss you, though."

"Hey, I'll be around, and then you can let me know where you go when you leave here. I'll move my stuff out after the sale tomorrow."

"Okay. You've been a great friend. Without you and your muscles, Plants-to-Go would never have gotten as far as it did."

"About Cantrell. My advice to you is—"

"Hush. Anyone living with someone named Debbie Mary Sue is in no position to express opinions about anything."

The afternoon passed quickly as Ashley finished tagging the plants with color-coded stickers to indicate their prices. After a light dinner, she contemplated the evening ahead and saw it as nothing more than a long stretch of empty hours.

Ryder, who was never far from her mind, instantly took front-row center. What was he doing in Austin? she wondered. Now, at that very moment, was he out with the construction crew, having a high old time? Was he resting? Maybe he was in a meeting, trying to solve whatever problems had brought him there. How was his shoulder? Was he thinking of her?

"Come home, Ryder," she said softly. "Come home and smile at me. See the doctor, like you're supposed to, and tell me everything is fine. Then I'll listen while you talk about your entire life." Oh, wonderful, she thought. She was no longer playing with a full deck.

Ashley was awake at dawn the next morning, and a grumbling Josh shuffled into the kitchen a short time later. Ashley shoved a mug of coffee into his hands and told him to hustle it up.

At seven o'clock sharp they opened the door to the warehouse.

At eight that night they closed it

Every plant in the place had been sold.

There had been a steady stream of customers, and Ashley and Josh had been busy keeping up with the traffic. As the inventory of plants decreased, Ashley more than once had had to blink away her tears as the realization that her dream was over struck her time and again. She would not, she decided firmly, allow herself to become depressed. Plants-to-Go no longer existed, but she had her future to think of.

"We could rent it out as a skating rink," Josh said, circling Ashley's shoulders with his arm. "Are you sad?"

"A little. I'm definitely out of business. Well,

there's no use crying any more tears over it. I'll use the rest of the time I have left to look for an apartment and a job. Three weeks should be long enough to get squared away."

"Well, I'm off to my new abode. Debbie Mary Sue awaits. I'll see you soon."

"Thank you for everything, Josh," Ashley said, hugging him tightly. "I really mean that."

"You betcha, kid."

A short time later, Ashley was alone in the warehouse. She wandered through the rows of troughs and picked an errant leaf off the floor, stroking it gently with her fingertip. The building was empty, suddenly cold, and she felt incredibly alone. Shutting off the fluorescent lights, she sank onto the chair at the desk and stared into the gloom. The soft glow from the desk lamp made eerie shadows that flickered over a few feet of the floor, and she felt as though she were caught in a cage, held captive within the circle of light. Water dripped steadily from a leaky faucet, and the sound seemed to pound against her temples. She wanted to run, but knew there was nowhere to go.

A sharp knock at the door caused her to gasp, and she gripped the edge of the desk until her knuckles turned white. She was frozen, unable to move, until the noise came again. She jumped to her feet and hurried to the door.

"Ryder! Oh, Ryder," she cried when she flung the door open. She hurled herself into his arms.

"Ashley, hey, what's wrong?"

"Nothing. Everything. Oh, goodness, you're home!"

"Yeah." He chuckled. "I'm home."

"And I'm glad," she said, smiling up at him.

"Lord, I missed you," he said, and claimed her mouth in a long, searing kiss.

And now *she* was home, too, Ashley thought dreamily as she circled Ryder's neck with her arms to hold him close. There, in the strong, protective embrace of Ryder Cantrell, was where she belonged.

"I have never," he said, close to her lips, "missed"—he kissed her—"anyone before when"—he kissed her again—"I went out of town."

"You haven't?" she asked breathlessly.

"No," he said, and took possession of her mouth once more.

His hands slid down the rounded slope of her buttocks and pressed her firmly against him. His arousal was evident as their bodies molded together, and Ashley relished the feel of his manhood and the knowledge that he wanted her. Desire swept through her like a brush fire. He caressed her back, then his hands moved to the sides of her breasts. They responded instantly, seeming to swell with need, the nipples hardening. Ryder's breathing became raspy and a soft moan came from Ashley's throat as their passions heightened.

"Ashley," Ryder said, taking a ragged breath, "I want you so much. I couldn't get you out of my mind while I was away. I have never desired a woman the way I do you."

"Oh, Ryder."

"No. No, this is wrong," he said, moving gently away from her. "This isn't the time or the place."

Yes, it was! Ashley thought wildly. Yes, yes, it was!

She loved him!

Somewhere in the middle of the whole chaotic mess she had fallen in love with Ryder. She wanted him to make love to her, to bring the promise of his masculinity to her and consume her with ecstasy. It didn't matter that he didn't love her. She loved him, and knew with a strange inner calmness that she would give herself to this man and suffer no regrets.

"Ryder . . ."

"There's water dripping in here somewhere."

"What?" She frowned. She was about to offer herself to him and he was talking about leaky faucets?

"It's a spigot that doesn't turn off tightly," she said. "It just sounds loud because the warehouse is empty. Ryder, I—"

"Empty? What do you mean, empty?"

"I had the sale today and—"

Ryder turned and flicked on the light switch by the door, flooding the room with brightness and causing Ashley to blink.

"Damn," he said, walking slowly past her, "everything is gone. Everything. Why did you move so fast on all of this?"

"You know I have to get out of here."

"Yeah, but you could have waited, and not gone crazy. I know a lot of people in Houston, and I might have been able to find you a building you could afford. Hell, now you don't even have any plants!"

"I chose to do it this way," she said, her voice rising slightly. "Plants-to-Go is my business, and the decisions are mine to make."

"Oh?" he said, turning to face her as he lit a cigarette. "And what's your next move?"

"I have three weeks to find a job and a place to live. I couldn't do everything at the same time, Ryder. It's better this way, having Plants-to-Go completely finished. Josh has already gone and—"

"Muscle-boy left you here alone?" Ryder bellowed. "Where in the hell did he go?"

"Debbie Mary Sue has an apartment and—"

"He's living with three women? Figures. He has delusions of grandeur about *everything*."

"No! That's her name."

"And he just up and takes a walk. Nice friend. You have no protection down here. Ashley, I could break in that door by leaning my shoulder against it. I'd like to wring that Josh's neck!"

Ryder's shoulder! Ashley thought suddenly. She hadn't even considered it when she went leaping into his arms. And he looked tired, really exhausted.

"Ryder, look, I—"

"You didn't use your head! If you advertised a going-out-of-business sale you were announcing that this place is empty. Every wino in the city will figure it's a great place to crash. Why in the hell didn't you wait until I got back, so I could—"

"You could what?" she yelled. "Tell me what to do? Watch over me as though I were your little sister, like Lucy? No, thank you, Ryder Cantrell. I don't need a baby-sitter. I'll do what I damn well please, and you have absolutely nothing to say about it."

Ryder's jaw tightened, and his eyes seemed to flash like emerald laser beams. Ashley stared at him, hoping to heaven that she looked more confident than she felt. He ground the cigarette out under the heel of his boot and walked slowly toward her. A roaring noise filled Ashley's head.

"Pack a suitcase," he ordered, his voice ominously low.

"What for?"

"You're coming with me. I'm not leaving you here."

"I am not budging," she said, crossing her arms over her breasts.

Ryder let out a long breath, took off his Stetson, raked his hand through his hair, and tugged the hat roughly back into place.

"You . . . are . . . driving me nuts," he said through clenched teeth.

"So, go home."

"I will say this once more." He spoke slowly. "You are not staying alone in this dump. I am tired, need about forty-two hours of sleep, and I'm in no mood to mess with you. You can come quietly or be carried out of here. Take your pick."

"You have no right to order me around."

"And you have no right to haunt me day and night," he yelled, causing her eyes to widen. "Or to pop into my head when I'm supposed to be concentrating on other things. You have no right to turn my life upside-down and make me ache with wanting you, but, by damn, you're doing it! I'm going to haul you out of here if I have to, but you're coming with me. I'm hungry, exhausted, I need a shower, and my shoulder hurts like hell. I don't need this hassle!"

"Your shoulder hurts?"

"Yeah, dammit, it does, and you're not helping any by standing there with your nose in the air, playing stubborn games. I want to go home and get some sleep. Get packed. Now! I said, now, Ashley!"

"You are pushy and arrogant and . . ."

"And?"

"I'm going to go pack," and she stomped off.

"I should hope so," he muttered. He was going to end up strangling that woman! he thought fiercely. But she had felt so good in his arms when he'd come through that door. She fit next to his body as if she'd been custom-made just for him. He'd meant it when he said he'd missed her while he was in Austin. It had jarred him at first, and then he had rather liked the idea that she'd be there waiting when he got back. He wanted to make love to her. Damn, even the thought of it was enough to arouse him. She was a virgin, though, he was sure of it, and that was a helluva responsibility for him to take on. Ah, hell, what was he going to do about Ashley Hunt? She was definitely, *definitely*, driving him nuts! And she was absolutely the cutest, most delectable woman he had ever seen.

"I'm ready to go, Mr. Bully," Ashley said, reappearing with a small suitcase in one hand.

"Fine."

"Except, where are we going?"

"My place. I'm too tired to drive out to the ranch, where Lucy and Pappy can chaperone. You'll just have to grin and bear it."

"Oh." Why was it that she always made brilliant statements like "Oh"? she wondered, shaking her head.

The drive to Ryder's apartment was made in total silence. He smoked one cigarette after another, and Ashley could virtually feel the tension between them crackling in the air. Her anger turned to sympathy and concern, however, when she saw him rotate his neck in a gesture of fatigue and absently rub his shoulder.

Tired and aching, Ryder had come to see her instead of going straight home, she thought. And he had missed her. Her! Granted, he had no business hollering his head off about her decisions regarding Plants-to-Go, but still . . . Oh, heavens, she loved him so much. He had a short fuse, a rotten temper, was stubborn, and threw a fit when he didn't get his own way. And she adored him. But, darn it, he was not going to treat her like a little sister who needed watching over. No, sir, she was a woman, and he'd better not forget it. Not that he'd had much problem remembering that when he'd come walking through her door. Goodness! He'd kissed the living daylights out of her. Oh, yes, she did love Ryder Cantrell.

When they reached his apartment, Ryder tossed his Stetson onto a chair and poured himself a stiff drink. He downed it in a single gulp and, without looking at Ashley, who was still standing by the door, strode into the bedroom. He returned with a blanket and pillow, dumped them onto the sofa, then sat down and tugged off his boots.

"You can have the bedroom," he said gruffly.

"Ryder, no. You're exhausted. Sleep in your own bed."

"Do you get some nutsy pleasure out of arguing about everything?"

"Me! You're the one who barks orders and expects everyone to jump. I've really had it with your telling me what to do, Ryder Cantrell. Maybe you're used to women who bat their eyelashes at you and swoon when you walk into the room, but I'm not one of them. Okay, now, you just listen. Go take that shower you wanted, while I fix you something to eat. Move your tush, Cantrell!"

Ryder looked at her for a long moment with a deep frown on his face. Then he pushed himself slowly to his feet, and Ashley wondered frantically if anyone would miss her after she had been murdered.

"Okay," he said calmly. "I think I'd like an omelet. Oh, and lots of toast and good, strong coffee. Also, slice up a couple of peaches into a bowl and pour some milk on them. Add a little sugar, not much, just a sprinkle. And could you hurry it up? I really do need to get some sleep."

"Uh . . ."

"I'll take a quick shower," he added, and strode from the room.

Had that gone right? Ashley thought. Why did she get the sneaky feeling that she'd been had?

She hummed softly as she prepared Ryder's meal. She felt at home in his kitchen, moving among his things. The aroma of soap reached her before she actually heard him approach, and she spun around, colliding with a rock-hard chest. A bare rock-hard chest. Her eyes were riveted to the curly mass of tawny hair and the taut bronzed skin beneath. She somehow registered the fact that Ryder was wearing jeans slung low on his hips and that there was a yellow towel draped around his neck. She lifted her eyes slowly, her gaze drifting past the strong column of Ryder's throat, on to the firm chin, the sensuous lips, straight nose, until she found herself staring into emerald eyes, which were radiating a warmth that melted her heart.

"Hello," Ryder said quietly, "fancy meeting you here."

"Your—your dinner is almost ready."

"That's nice," he said absently.

They didn't touch or speak. In fact, they hardly breathed. They simply drank in the sight of the other. Seconds that could have been hours passed, and then Ryder lifted his hand and placed it gently on Ashley's cheek. The green of his eyes took on the smoky hue of desire, and still they did not touch, except for the work-roughened hand on the velvet-soft cheek. It was a timeless moment of discovery, of sharpened awareness. Though the air was filled with the scents of toast and coffee and soapy freshness, neither noticed anything but the other.

"Welcome home, Ryder," Ashley finally whispered.

He simply nodded, then lowered his head and kissed her.

Five

Ryder brushed his lips across Ashley's, but as he reached out his arms to gather her into his embrace, he stiffened.

"I hate to say this," he stated, "but I think my kitchen is on fire."

"Oh, Lord, the omelet!" Ashley shrieked.

Ryder whipped the towel from his neck and wrapped it around the handle of the flaming frying pan. He tossed it all into the sink and doused it with water.

"Whew!" he exclaimed, fanning the air with his hands.

"Do you have another frying pan?" Ashley asked weakly. "I'll start over."

"Yeah, there's one in the cupboard someplace."

"Oh, Ryder," she said softly, "your shoulder."

Ryder glanced down at the long, jagged scar, which had been covered by the towel.

"Pretty, huh?" he said. "I'm embroidered."

She lifted her hand to touch the injured area, then hesitated. He covered her hand with his and pressed it against the warm skin.

"It's a part of me, Ashley." He spoke quietly. "It isn't going to go away. Did Lucy tell you what happened?"

"Yes, she did." She was agonizingly aware of the heat from Ryder's body. "She told me about Jimmy. It's all so sad, Ryder."

"But it's over. That's what Lucy has got to understand. Maybe she'll get a handle on it, now that she's talked to you."

"I hope so. But it really isn't over. You can't hide the fact that your shoulder is bothering you. You're in pain and—"

"And I'm going to be in a lot more pain if I don't get something to eat," he said, smiling at her. "I'm a starving man."

"Oh, Ryder." She sighed. "Why do you do that? Why do you skitter around the edges of anything remotely close to you and leave me standing on the outside? Just when I think we might be getting closer, you pull away, move back behind an invisible wall that I can't get through. You said you missed me, yet I'm here now and you're still keeping me at arm's length. Tell me about your shoulder, Ryder. Tell me exactly what you think is wrong with it. And Pappy. What about him? What's the long story you refuse to share? Oh, please, Ryder, talk to me."

A flicker of anger crossed Ryder's face, and then a strange, haunting pain seemed to settle in the depth of his eyes. He raked his hand through his hair and appeared to be struggling within himself, waging a battle in his mind and soul. Ashley watched him anxiously, silently willing him to speak, to tell her who he was, how he felt.

"Don't push me," he said finally, his voice low.

"Accept who I am, the way I am. I thought you were different. You seem so honest and real."

"I am!"

"And now you're making demands, shoving me against the wall, telling me how I should perform to meet your standards. I won't strip my soul bare for you, Ashley. Not for you or anyone. Not ever! If you don't accept that right now, then you and I don't stand a chance in hell of making it. I— Ah, hell!" He reached out and pulled her roughly into his arms. "Don't make me pass tests for you."

"Oh, Ryder."

"Ashley, I'm tired. I don't mean because I need some sleep. I'm tired of fighting so damn hard for everything. All my life I've had to fight. Please, babe, just look at me as a man, nothing more, and don't try to change me, mold me into what you'd have me be."

"I'm so sorry. I didn't mean to try to—"

Ryder tilted her chin up and covered her mouth hard with his. A sob caught in Ashley's throat and she wrapped her arms around his waist. Her fingers spread like fans on his back, and she could feel his heat, the muscles moving under her touch. His tongue sought and found hers, sending shock waves of desire swirling through her. Her breasts were crushed against his chest as he gathered her even closer and the kiss went on and on. Their mouths ravished each other's with frenzied, urgent motions, until Ryder finally lifted his head.

"I think," he said, his voice raspy, "we'd better have some dinner. I'll go put on a shirt."

He looked at her, his eyes cloudy with desire, then ran his hands gently down her arms to catch her fingers. He brought each to his mouth for a fleeting kiss before turning and leaving the room.

Ashley stared after him, her knees trembling and her heart beating wildly. Her mind was whirling from his passionately spoken words. Accept him as he was or not at all, that was her choice. But she had no choice. It was too late for that, because she loved him. Ryder cared for her, she knew he did. But love her? No, he had never said that. And now he had made it clear that his secrets were his to keep, that he had no intention of sharing his inner self.

Oh, dear heaven, why did it have to be this way? She had pictured love as a joining not only of bodies but of hearts and minds and souls as well. The giving and receiving was to have been complete, total. But not so with Ryder Cantrell. She would get only the portion of himself that he carefully chose to give her. Could she live that way? Be happy? What difference did it make? She was committed to him because she loved him. She would take what he offered and cherish it, holding on to it as a precious treasure. She couldn't leave Ryder, even though he didn't return her love. She couldn't look further for someone who would give totally of himself. She would stay for as long as he wanted her. Her pride be damned.

Ashley brushed a tear from her cheek and found another frying pan in the cupboard. As she began to break eggs into a bowl, Ryder came up behind her and kissed her on the cheek.

"The toast is cold," he said. "I'll make some more. You're going to eat, too, aren't you?"

"I guess so. Josh and I were busy with the sale, and we didn't have time to stop to eat."

"Then you're definitely having some of this."

Ashley looked at Ryder out of the corner of her eye and saw that he had pulled on, but not buttoned, a western shirt. The sleeves were rolled back on his tanned forearms and the shirt hung loose from his pants. His feet were still bare. He moved around the kitchen with graceful ease.

There they were, she thought, she and Ryder,

making dinner in the kitchen. The scene was ordinary, but everything seemed foreign to her. She had changed because of this man. She was in love for the first time in her life, and felt split in two. The rush of happiness she felt when Ryder walked into the room was hers, but not the man. She'd have to settle for so much less than she'd dreamed of having.

"So be it," she murmured.

"So be what?" Ryder asked.

"Nothing. I didn't realize I had spoken out loud. Toast ready? Here come the eggs."

They ate in silence for several minutes. Then Ryder reached across the table and took Ashley's hand.

"Do I ask too much?" he said softly. "I am who I am, Ashley, but maybe that means I'll never have a chance to have someone like you in my life."

"No, Ryder, you don't ask too much. At least you're honest. You have walls around you that are solid, and all I can do is walk through the doors you choose to open. I'll try not to ask more of you than you're capable of giving."

"Thank you. Oh, Ashley, thank you. You knocked me over the minute I saw you. I don't want to lose you without knowing what we might come to have together. But now we have a chance to find out. Together. All right?"

"Yes," she whispered.

"Hey," he said, grinning at her, "you sold all your plants, and you were supposed to fancy up my office."

"Sir, your reception area is a spectacle of beauty," she said, forcing a smile.

She rattled off the scientific names for the plants she had taken to Cantrell Construction, and laughed when Ryder insisted she repeat everything in English. The tension between them slowly lifted and was replaced by banter and teasing. A small section of

Ashley's heart, however, sorrowed for what might have been but would never be. A part of the man, though, she told herself, was better than none at all.

Ryder smoked a cigarette, then helped load the dishwasher, chuckling when Ashley gasped as he threw the burned frying pan into the trash. The kitchen set to order, they walked back into the living room, where Ryder sat down on the sofa and patted the cushion next to him.

"Come here," he said.

"You need to get some sleep," she reminded him, sitting beside him.

"I will."

"Did you solve the problems in Austin?"

"Yep." He circled her shoulders with his arm. "We geniuses just move in and get the job done."

She laughed. "Do tell."

"Certainly. Take, for example, the fact that I have a very lovely woman curled up next to me here. What would someone of my superior intelligence do in a case like this?"

"I have no idea."

"Oh? Well, I'll show you," he said, shifting slightly to face her. "The first thing would be to fulfill my fantasy about that ebony waterfall of hair."

He lifted her braid and tugged the rubber band from the end. With gentle motions he pulled the tresses loose, raking the tangles free with his fingers.

Ashley was hardly breathing as he drew her hair forward and watched it slide like silken threads through his fingers to fall heavily over her breasts.

"Beautiful," he murmured. "Incredibly beautiful."

Their eyes met and held in a timeless moment. There was no passion in Ryder's eyes. It seemed to Ashley that he was trying to memorize her every feature. As if of their own volition, her fingers moved to rest gently on his cheek. He turned his head slightly to place his lips on her palm. The sensuous softness caused desire to surge through her, and she swallowed heavily as her heart raced.

"I want to make love to you, Ashley Hunt," Ryder said, his voice oddly husky. "I desire you more than any woman I have ever known. But, Ashley, we can't decide together when the moment is right because I want you now, this minute. It's going to have to be up to you. Maybe that's putting a heavy burden on you, but I don't know what else to do. I know you respond to me, but I can't read your emotions and I don't know what you can handle. Ashley, have you ever been with a man?"

"No," she said, her voice hardly above a whisper as she dropped her hand from his face.

"I didn't think you had. I sensed it. We'll be fantastic together, I promise you. But please, babe, don't do anything you're not mentally prepared for. There's no room for regrets with something like this. I'm asking you for the greatest gift you have to give a man, and you have every right to say no. I'll understand, believe me. I care for you, Ashley, I truly, truly do. You've become very special to me very quickly. Because of that, I want, *need*, you to be sure."

Ashley looked into Ryder's eyes and saw tenderness there, a gentleness, an understanding. Her heart nearly burst with love for this man, for his sensitivity and willingness to allow her to follow her heart. She felt cherished, like something fragile and precious, which Ryder would not touch before she declared herself ready.

A stillness washed over her as she gazed at him. In that quiet moment she looked deep within herself and knew with every fiber of her being that the time had arrived. She would cross over into a new and different place, but would not make the journey alone. Ryder would be there. Her Ryder.

She lifted her hand and placed it on his bare chest, feeling the steady beating of his heart. Unexpectedly tears sprang to her eyes, and her voice was a hushed whisper.

"Make love to me, Ryder," she said.

"Are you really sure?"

"Yes."

"Ah, Ashley." He gathered her close and held her tightly. "Thank you. Thank you for giving me this much, for trusting me this much. It means more to me than I can tell you."

Ryder lifted her into his arms and pushed himself up. He carried her into the bedroom, pulled back the blankets on the bed, and laid her gently down. He dropped his shirt to the floor, then stretched out next to her.

"Are you frightened?" he asked softly.

"No," she said, drinking in the sight of his glistening torso in the dim luminescence from the lamp on the nightstand.

"I'll try not to hurt you, Ashley, but the first time isn't always very good. We'll have all night. It will be wonderful, I promise."

He gently removed her clothing, his breath quickening at the sight of her naked splendor. Then his lips and tongue and hands began a languorous, tantalizing journey over her body. Ashley trembled beneath his touch, closing her eyes to savor every pleasurable sensation he created. Her hands trailed over his back, and she gloried in the feel of his hot, smooth skin and powerful muscles.

Ryder placed fluttering kisses over her breasts, then drew one rosy bud into his mouth. She gasped as her passion burst into a raging flame. He moved to the other breast when she began to shift restlessly, aching with a need that was new but not frightening.

"Oh, Ryder," she said, "I feel so . . . I . . . ."

"You're so lovely, so soft," he said huskily. Dear Lord, how he wanted her, he thought, but she was so small, like a china doll. He couldn't, *wouldn't,* hurt her—but what if he did? She was giving him so much, and it had to be perfect for her. This was Ashley. Ashley! "Oh, babe," he murmured, burying his face in the fragrant cloud of her hair as he strove for control.

He turned and slid off the bed to shed his clothing, hesitating as he saw Ashley's expression of wonder as her gaze flickered over his body. He stood quietly, waiting, allowing her to know him and what would be hers. His manhood was a bold announcement of his need, and he searched her face for fear, but saw none. He let out a rush of breath as she lifted her hand to him, only then realizing he had hardly been breathing.

He lay down next to her again and claimed her mouth, his tongue delving deep. His hand caressed her breasts, moved to the flat plane of her stomach, and on to the warmth between her thighs.

"Ryder," she gasped. "Oh, please."

He reached into the nightstand drawer and quickly prepared himself. Moving over her, he hesitated, resting on his arms as he gazed down at her passion-flushed face. He felt a tightness in his throat as she smiled at him tenderly, trustingly, and then he entered her. Ashley's sharp cry of pain seemed to rip at his very soul, and he gritted his teeth, waiting until he felt her relax beneath him once again.

And then it began. The ritual as ancient as humankind itself became a rapturous celebration only for them. Ashley was swept away by powerful waves of ecstasy, and arched her back to bring him closer yet. She felt him carrying her beyond this world, and it was glorious. He was leading her to an unknown treasure, and she had to find it. She had to!

"Ryder!" she cried out as she seemed to shatter into a million exploding colors.

"Yes." He groaned, joining her, sharing the treasure at the journey's end.

He collapsed against her, and she relished his crushing weight, holding him tightly. He pushed himself up to rest on his arms and looked at her anxiously.

"I hurt you," he said.

"Ryder, no. It was everything you promised—and more. I never dreamed it would be so . . . I didn't know . . . Oh, Ryder, it was wonderful."

He kissed her long and hard, then moved gently away and pulled her close to his side.

"Thank you," he said, his lips resting on her forehead. "I don't know what else to say. You gave of yourself totally and . . . Thank you."

He drew the blankets up around them, then sank back against the pillow with a weary sigh.

"You're so tired," Ashley said.

"No, I'm fine. I . . . really . . . am."

She looked at him and realized to her amazement that he was sound asleep. With a smile on her lips she snuggled close to his body and shut her eyes, drifting off into a contented slumber.

Something woke Ashley from a deep, dreamless sleep and she blinked in confusion, not comprehending where she was. The light was still on and the clock on the nightstand read just after three A.M. When Ryder moaned she knew what had wakened her, and she sat up, looking at him with concern. His hand was gripping his shoulder, and his face and chest were wet with perspiration. His thick hair was tousled and moist, and he was moving his head restlessly on the pillow. He appeared still to be asleep, and Ashley chewed her bottom lip nervously, not knowing what to do. He was obviously in pain, but should she wake him? Leave him alone? Was this one of those private places into which she had been forbidden to tread?

"Damn," he muttered as he dug his fingers into his shoulder, but still did not open his eyes.

"That's it," she said firmly. "Ryder, wake up. Ryder!"

"What!" he exclaimed, sitting bolt upright and nearly colliding with her head-on. "What's wrong? Ashley? Yes, it's you. What's wrong?"

"Nothing," she answered, flopping back onto the pillow. "I just thought I'd say hello."

"Huh?"

"Now that you're awake, you might notice that you're dripping with sweat because your shoulder is killing you. I just figured I'd mention it." She closed her eyes.

"You are weird!"

"Good night," she said pleasantly.

"I think I'll take some aspirin," he said, getting out of the bed.

"Whatever you want," she said, peering at him with one eye as he walked into the bathroom. Gotcha, Cantrell, she thought smugly. Score one for the kid who grows plants.

Ryder came back into the bedroom and turned off the light before sliding back into bed. A chuckle rumbled up from his chest as he reached for Ashley's hand and gave it a gentle squeeze.

"Nicely done, clever lady," he said.

"What?" she asked innocently.

"I like you, Ashley Hunt. I like you a whole helluva lot."

She smiled. "Good night, Ryder."

When Ashley woke again, the bedroom was flooded with sunlight and the clock said eight A.M. She glanced quickly at Ryder, who was deeply asleep, one arm thrown over his eyes. There was a healthy growth of tawny beard on his face, and Ashley decided instantly that he was beautiful. As she shifted slightly, her body complained of a foreign soreness. She welcomed each sensation and relived in her mind the exquisite details of her lovemaking with Ryder.

She had no regrets. She had given herself to the only man she had ever loved, and now she was his. And Ryder? He would give as much of himself as he was able. She didn't know for how long, nor at that point did she care. She would live for now. The future be damned. Each moment, each precious, precious moment with this man, would be stored away in her heart.

A large hand sliding across her stomach caused Ashley to jump in surprise, and she turned her head to find herself nose to nose with Ryder.

"Hi," he said. "How are you?"

She smiled. "Fine."

"Probably not. Have you tried to move yet?"

"Sort of."

"Well"—he nuzzled her neck—"don't be upset if you're a little sore here and there."

"Here and there?" she asked, her breath catching as his hand slid upward to cup one firm breast.

"There and here." He placed a ribbon of kisses down her slender neck. "Your hair is so gorgeous spread out on that pillow, but I knew it would be. But I've got to get out of this bed."

"Why?"

"Because you don't need me all over you until

you've had time to recuperate. I hurt you once, and I don't intend to do it again. I'll wait."

"You're so considerate, Ryder," she said, trailing a finger down his chest. "You really are."

"Don't do that!"

"Do what?" she asked, sliding lower and drawing lazy circles on his chest with her tongue.

"Oh, Lord," he moaned.

"I recuperate very quickly."

He chuckled. "You also learn very quickly. Give me a break. I'm trying to be a nice guy."

"Love me, Ryder," she whispered.

"Ah, Ashley," he said, weaving his fingers through her hair, "you're telling me so much. You're not sorry. You don't regret giving yourself to me."

"No. No, I don't. I'll cherish last night forever. You made it so beautiful for me. I'm glad, so very glad, that I waited for you, Ryder."

"Ashley," he said with a growl, and took fierce possession of her mouth.

He stroked and kissed and caressed and loved her with his lips and hands, until she was begging him to take her. Her hands traveled across his rugged contours, exploring, seeking, finding, and bringing him to a height of trembling passion. They came together at last, their bodies moving together in the wondrous dance known only to lovers, until rapture exploded within them and they cried out each other's names. As their heartbeats quieted and their breathing returned to normal, neither spoke. They lay entwined, hands resting on each other in gentle possessiveness, and savored the contentment that enveloped them.

"So special," Ryder finally said. "You are, you know."

"I'm glad you think so."

"Would you like to go out to the ranch with me?"

"When?"

"Now. Well, after a shower, some clothes on the bodies, and breakfast."

"Marvelous."

"Then, up," he said, swinging his feet to the floor. "The day awaits."

Ashley snuggled deeper into the blankets while Ryder showered, and was nearly asleep when he reentered the room, clad only in a towel draped low on his hips.

"Your turn," he said.

Ashley flushed with embarrassment as she realized she was about to walk naked across the room in full view of Ryder. It was ridiculous, and she knew it, but still she hesitated. This was Ryder, the man she loved, the man she had given herself to with no shame.

"To hear the shout of whispers," he said quietly.

"Pardon me?"

He walked over to the bed and sat down next to her, picking up her hand and gently kissing the palm.

"I haven't thought of that saying in years," he said. "Pappy explained it to me a long time ago. It means that sometimes people's actions and words are so subtle or quiet they're like whispers. But actually a message, something important, is being shouted. When you care about someone, really care, you pay attention to the whispers being shouted. You made me remember."

He reached to the floor for his discarded shirt and handed it to Ashley, smiled tenderly, then walked to the dresser. He turned his back to her while she slipped the shirt on and hurried into the bathroom.

In the shower, Ashley blinked away her tears and allowed the water to beat against her body. To hear the shout of whispers, she thought. What a beautiful way to phrase it. And Ryder had done that for her. He had sensed her sudden, foolish embarrassment as though she had shouted it across the room, and he had understood. Oh, dear heaven, how she loved him.

Her breasts were sore from her lovemaking with Ryder, and the "here and there" he had made reference to also complained, but she relished each sensation. She felt alive and feminine and complete. Even if Ryder didn't love her, she knew he cared for her. Maybe if she watched, listened, for the shout of his whispers, she would learn more about this man, who protected his inner self so rigidly against those who would seek entry. Maybe.

Ryder was not in the bedroom when she returned, and she dressed quickly in jeans and a plaid cotton shirt. The aroma of coffee drifted through the air, and she headed for the kitchen. Ryder was standing by the stove in faded jeans and a black western shirt that pulled tightly across his broad shoulders. The jeans hugged his hips and molded his muscular thighs, and Ashley's heart was racing as she walked to his side.

"Good," he said, kissing her quickly. "You left your hair loose."

"I just haven't braided it yet."

"No, leave it."

"It will get all tangled."

"I'll brush it for you. Leave it."

She smiled. "Do you always get your own way?"

"I sure as hell try," he answered with a grin. "You are toast. I'm eggs. Since this is the last frying pan I own, we've traded jobs."

Ashley poked him in the ribs and made the toast.

"Tasty," Ryder said when they had finished. He lit a cigarette and squinted against the rising smoke as he exhaled. Then he reached across the table and lifted a handful of Ashley's hair, watching as it sifted through his fingers. "Incredible," he murmured.

"Do you have a hair fetish?"

Ryder whooped in delight and shook his head.

"You're something," he said. "I never know what you're going to say. You keep a man on his toes. You also have a helluva temper, of which I was the recipient the day you marched onto my construction site. You're a scary lady."

"Bull."

"You're also"—he was suddenly serious—"a very passionate, very desirable woman. And, Ashley? You are mine. I don't share. I think we'd better reach an understanding about that right now and avoid any trouble. You are my lady. I was your first lover, and no man—no man, Ashley—is going to touch you while I'm on the scene. I intend to protect you, take care of you. Do you have a problem with that?"

Lord, she thought, how macho and pushy and arrogant and borderline nervy. And how absolutely marvelous. "No, I have no problem with that at all," she said. "But I assume this works both ways?"

"Yep." He smiled. "We're going steady. How's that?"

"Quaint."

"It has class. Let's clean up this mess and hit the road."

The Texas sky was clear and blue, with only an errant cloud dotting its vibrant color. The citizens of Houston were out and about, some heading for church, others prepared to spend the day out of doors in the cool spring air. The heat would come with the beginning of summer, baking the soil, forcing people to go back inside, but now the weather was perfect.

Ryder explained that the ranch was ten miles out of town and had once been part of an enormous stretch of land that belonged to an oil man. Ryder had convinced the millionaire to sell a small section on the edge of the property to him, which Ryder had fenced and then built a house on. He ran a few head of cattle and some horses, but did not consider it a working ranch.

"The Triple C is just there," he said as they drove through town in the truck. "I have a foreman who takes care of everything, and he hires extra hands if something needs doing. His wife is the housekeeper. It's just a nice, quiet place for getting away from the noise of the city. Pappy is in seventh heaven out there and Lucy is content enough."

"You call it the Triple C?"

"Yeah, well, that's for me, Lucy, and Pappy. Pappy's last name is McKenzie, but I think of him as a Cantrell."

"That's nice," Ashley said. But who *was* Pappy? she wanted to know. And where did he fit into the picture? Well, she knew better than to ask. She was also wondering about Ryder's shoulder. He'd made no mention of the scene in the middle of the night, nor had he massaged it this morning. Was it still bothering him, and he was just being careful not to draw attention to it? Or had the rest he had gotten eased the pain? Oh, damn the man and his secrets, his stubbornness. He was enough to give her the crazies!

After leaving the city, Ryder drove along a narrow paved road, then turned onto a dirt road. After they'd traveled several more miles, he pointed out the right window.

"There she is," he said. "The Triple C."

The house was a single-story ranch-style, with a white exterior and a red tile roof, which gave it a Spanish flair. It was fairly large and had a wide porch across the front. Ryder stopped by the steps and Ashley slid out of the truck.

"It's lovely," she said.

"Lucy decorated it," he said, coming around to join her. "She can give you a tour. Listen, she's going to be all over me about my shoulder, so just ignore her until she's done hollering. She can be a real shrew sometimes."

"She loves you, Ryder."

"Hell, I know that, but she doesn't have to be so loud about it. Let's go in."

The Spanish motif had been carried over to the inside of the house, with hardwood floors, and bright rugs hanging on the stark white walls. Woven baskets held an array of dried flowers, and the furniture was hand-carved, dark, and heavy. The overall effect was striking and welcoming, and Ashley raved on and on as she wandered around the huge living room.

"I'm glad you like it," Ryder said, smiling. "I wonder where everyone is."

"Well, look who's here," Pappy said. He seemed to have materialized out of nowhere. " 'Bout time you came out here, boy. Howdy, missy."

"Hello, Pappy," Ashley said.

"How's that patience comin'?" Pappy asked.

"Slowly but surely."

He nodded. "Fair enough."

"Where's Lucy?" Ryder asked.

"Not here."

"Obviously. So where is she?"

"Out."

Ryder looked at the ceiling for a long moment, and took a deep breath.

"Okay," he said, "I'll play your dumb game. Pappy, I have this sister named Lucy, ya know? She lives here. If it wouldn't strain your brain too much, could you tell where said person is hiding?"

"You two had breakfast?" Pappy asked, causing Ashley to swallow a bubble of laughter.

"Dammit, Pappy!" Ryder roared.

"Calm yourself, boy. Lucy will be home soon, I imagine. She's in the city. Called me last night and said she was stayin' over."

"Staying over? Where? With who?"

"Seems to me she said his name was Brad," Pappy said thoughtfully. "Yep, Brad. That was it."

"Uh-oh," Ashley muttered.

"What did you say?" Ryder asked, his jaw tightening.

"Want some pancakes?" Pappy asked.

"Who in the hell is Brad?" Ryder bellowed. "Are you telling me that Lucy spent the night with a man?"

"What you're hearin', boy," Pappy said quietly, "is that Lucy is comin' out of her cocoon of grief, and she's long overdue. Jimmy is dead and buried, and your sister is alive. It's time, Ryder. Let her go. Love her enough to let her go. She might make some mistakes, but that's her right. She's like a baby takin' her first steps again, and she may stumble a few times. But she's our Lucy, and she's goin' to be fine. Don't ruin this for her, Ryder, or you'll answer to me. I haven't told you what to do in a mighty long while except for naggin' about your workin' too hard. But I mean it, boy. You leave Lucy be."

Ashley chewed on her lower lip as she anxiously watched Ryder's face. His eyes were cold and a pulse was beating in his neck. His stance was rigid, and he reminded her of a deadly panther about to pounce. Tension hung in the air as the two men stared at each other. Then Ryder drew a shuddering breath, as his shoulders gradually relaxed.

"We already had breakfast," he said slowly, his voice low, "but I'd never pass up your fresh-squeezed orange juice, Pappy."

Pappy nodded, then turned and left the room.

Tears clung to Ashley's lashes, and she swallowed the lump in her throat. With a soft moan Ryder pulled her roughly into his arms, burying his face in her hair as he held her tightly.

Six

"Ashley," Ryder finally said, "would you like some orange juice?"

"I'd love some orange juice." She smiled up at him.

He put his arm around her shoulders and led her from the room and down the hallway. Changes, he thought. So many, so quickly. Ashley was turning his world upside down and now Lucy was attempting to break free of the emotional chains that had held her captive for two years. The changes weren't bad or wrong, they were just happening, jarring him, making him edgy. He had never before told a woman that she was his and was to see no other man, as he had done with Ashley. But he had to! No one was going to touch her but him! Ah, hell, what was he doing? His mind was so screwed up.

"Oh, what a cheerful kitchen." Ashley's voice jarred Ryder out of his reverie.

"Maria keeps it spotless," Pappy said. "She and

John are off to church. Here's some juice and there's blueberry muffins. Sit."

Ashley and Ryder sat down at a glass-topped table in front of a large window that looked out on a breathtaking view of the rolling ranchland. Horses could be seen in corrals that were set off by gleaming white fences, and just beyond them was a red barn.

"Newborn kittens in the barn," Pappy said, joining them at the table.

"I'll walk Ashley down and show her," Ryder said. "Anything else going on around here I should know about?"

"Nope. John has it runnin' smooth as an oiled clock."

"This juice is delicious, Pappy," Ashley said. "I—"

"Hello, everyone," Lucy interrupted, suddenly appearing in the doorway.

Ashley looked quickly at Ryder, who had stiffened in his chair. A silence fell over the room as brother and sister stared at each other, and Ashley was sure they would hear the pounding of her heart. Pappy reached over and covered Ashley's hand with his dry, rough one, giving her a reassuring wink. Ryder pushed himself slowly to his feet and cleared his throat.

"Lucy," he said, "you're—you're just in time to join us for some orange juice."

"Oh, Ryder," Lucy cried, rushing into his arms and hugging him. "Thank you."

"Go slowly, Lucy," he said softly. "Go with my blessings, but do it right."

"I will," she promised, brushing tears off her cheeks.

"Oh-h-h," Ashley said as tears filled her own eyes. "Oh, dear me."

"Everybody's sprung a leak around here," Pappy said gruffly. "Blow your noses and sit down."

Lucy and Ryder slid into their chairs like obedient children. Ryder got up again an instant later, as the telephone rang.

"Cantrell," he said into the receiver. "Yeah. . . . No, I can't come in there today. . . . Okay, read me the figures."

"Ashley," Lucy said quietly, "I'm so glad to see you here. Ryder has never brought a woman to the ranch before. Never."

"I didn't know that," Ashley replied. *To hear the shout of whispers,* she thought. *It was one of those. It was!* "I feel very special."

"For good reason, I'd say," Pappy remarked.

"Pappy," Lucy said, "Ryder was so wonderful about my staying in town, and I'm sure I have you to thank for that. I hate to set him off now by mentioning his shoulder, but he's got to go see Dr. Metcalf."

"Leave it be for today," Pappy said. "That boy can be pushed just so far in a given number of hours. Count your blessin's and shut your mouth."

"But—"

"That's all, girl. Don't be naggin' him today."

Lucy sighed. "Okay."

"That goes for you, too, missy," Pappy added, causing Lucy to burst into laughter.

"What's the joke?" Ryder asked, hanging up the phone.

"Ashley's just finding out who's running this outfit," Lucy said.

"*I* am." Ryder swung his long leg over the chair and sat down.

"When hell freezes over, boy." Pappy cackled. "Yep, when hell freezes over."

Ryder grinned, and shrugged as though Pappy's declaration were not exactly a news flash, and they finished their snack with friendly banter.

"Kittens." Ryder pushed himself to his feet. "Who's coming?" he asked.

"I've seen 'em," Pappy said.

"Me too," added Lucy. "Oh, gosh, I guess you two will just have to go alone. Isn't that an awful shame?"

Ryder chuckled and shook his head as he extended his hand to Ashley, who was blushing. He squeezed her hand as they left the house. Inside the barn, he led her to a stall layered with fresh-smelling hay. When she saw the cluster of tiny, furry kittens, she dropped to her knees.

"Oh, they're adorable," she said, stroking the kittens' heads.

"Want one when they're old enough?" Ryder asked, hunkering down next to her.

"I'd love one, but I'll have to wait and see what the rules are about pets when I find an apartment."

He frowned. "What are you talking about?"

"You're plowing under my so-called house, remember? Oh, look, the kitten is sticking out its little tongue."

"Ashley, I thought we'd covered the subject of your being my lady now."

"We did," she said, looking at him in surprise. "We both agreed we wouldn't see other people."

"So what's this about your getting an apartment?"

"Ryder, you're confusing me."

"Look, I've never before asked anyone to see only me, because I didn't care that much what other women did. You are mine, and I'm sure as hell not walking you to your door and kissing you good night, nor am I dragging myself home at dawn in yesterday's clothes, as if this were an endless string of one-night stands. You'll live with me, at my apartment, and sleep in my bed every damn night of the week."

"What?" she whispered.

"What is this?" he asked, pushing himself to his

feet. "I thought you understood what I was saying to you."

"I guess I didn't." She looked up at him with wide eyes. "We never discussed living together!"

"I'm your lover, dammit! Where else would I want you to be?"

"Why don't you announce it to the whole world?" she retorted, scrambling to her feet. "Be quiet, for Pete's sake."

"No! Oh, man, you are making me mad!"

"Me! You're the one taking a lot for granted here. Living together is a very big step."

"So is what you did last night, or didn't that count for anything?" he snapped.

"That's it." Ashley pushed past him and stomped toward the barn door. "You are the rudest, most infuriating, the most—"

"Ashley, wait!"

"Take a hike, Cantrell!"

"Ah, hell!" he said, giving the stall a swift kick. "Ow! Dammit!"

Ashley marched back to the house with a determined tilt to her chin and entered the kitchen. Lucy and Pappy were still sitting at the table.

"If a very tall, very angry man comes in search of my person"—Ashley spoke to a spot on the far wall—"please inform him that I am not available for comment."

"Oh, no," Lucy said.

"Is that a bathroom I see?" Ashley asked. "Yes, it is. Fine. Thank you. Good-bye."

Pappy chuckled merrily as the bathroom door was firmly closed.

"Oh, Pappy," Lucy said, looking out of the window, "here comes Ryder, and I swear there's smoke billowing out of his ears. If I had any brains I'd get out of here, but I'd really hate to miss this."

Lucy covered her eyes with her hand as Ryder came barreling in the back door. Pappy simply gestured to the bathroom with his thumb, and Ryder covered the distance with three long, heavy strides.

"Ashley," he bellowed, "open this damn door!"

"No!"

"I'm going to kick it in if you don't come out of there!"

"Would he do that?" Lucy asked Pappy, peering between her fingers.

"Yep," Pappy said.

"Don't you have any respect for property?" Ashley asked, flinging the door open.

"Yes!" Ryder said, planting his hands on his hips. "I respect you, don't I?"

"I am not your property!"

"Yes, you are!"

"Did he say that?" Lucy shrieked. "Did he honestly say that?"

"Yep." Pappy nodded.

"I'd shoot him," Lucy said. "I really would."

"Will you people knock it off?" Ryder said. "I have a very angry woman on my hands here, and you're not helping one damn bit."

"Sorry," Lucy said. "I won't say another word."

"Ashley," Ryder began, "what we have here is a simple case of lack of communication. Now, then! We'll sit down and calmly discuss this like two mature adults. Okay?"

"Okay."

"Come on." He took her hand. "Let's go into the living room."

"Don't you yell at me again, Ryder Cantrell," Ashley said, "or I'll pop you in the chops."

"I understand perfectly," he said, leading her from the room.

"I don't believe it," Lucy whispered. "Was that my brother?"

"Yep." Pappy was shaking with laughter. "He's been knocked over by a butterfly."

"Amazing."

In the living room, Ryder pulled Ashley into his arms and kissed her so passionately she could hardly breathe.

"I'm sorry," he said when he finally ended the searing embrace. "I know last night was special, rare, beautiful. And, babe, I don't for one minute take you for granted. I want you with me. I don't understand what's happening here. All I know is, you've become very important to me. Give us a chance to find out what we have together. Live in my house, sleep in my bed, be my lady. Please, Ashley, do this for—for us."

"Oh, Ryder." She leaned her head against his chest.

Oh, Ashley, please! Ryder thought fiercely. Why was he doing this? Why? Nothing made sense anymore. But he needed this woman to be close to him, where he could touch her, hold her, take care of her.

Everything was happening so quickly, Ashley thought. She couldn't think straight any longer.

"Ashley," Ryder said softly, "remember what I said about hearing the shout of whispers?"

"Yes."

"I'm shouting, babe, so you know exactly what I'm saying. I need you with me. Be with me, please. Please, Ashley?"

"I need you, too, Ryder. I . . . Yes, I'll live in your home, and sleep in your bed, and—and be your lady."

"Ashley." He groaned, and took possession of her mouth in a long kiss.

She was lost, Ashley thought dreamily. Gone. Her senses spiraled to a fever pitch of desire when

Ryder parted her lips and sought her tongue with his. Any second thoughts or inner fears about the ramifications of living with Ryder were swept into a sea of oblivion.

"I think," he said, taking a ragged breath, "I'd better cool off before we get caught. Ashley, thank you."

He slowly moved away from her, then lifted her heavy hair and buried his face in its fragrance. Then he stepped back, lit a cigarette, and walked to the window as he strove for control.

Oh, what had she done? Ashley wondered, pressing her hands to her burning cheeks. She loved this man with every breath in her body and now was going to live with him day and night, be a part of his life, as though she were his wife. But for how long? And how would she bear the pain when it was over? He wanted her, and it was glorious that he had expressed his need for her so fiercely. But he still did not love her!

Ryder stared out at the tranquil setting and took a deep drag on his cigarette. Ashley was his, he thought. She was coming home with him. But how long would she stay? Which day, or night, would he reach for her and find her gone? He knew he was setting himself up to be ripped to shreds again, but he couldn't seem to stop himself. For as long as she was there, he would cherish and protect her, because—because he loved her. How long had he known it? How long had he denied what he knew was true? It didn't matter. It really didn't matter, because he had no intention of telling her.

He ground out his cigarette in an ashtray and turned to face Ashley.

"We'd better go back in the kitchen," he said, smiling slightly, "before Lucy faints from curiosity about what's been going on in here."

With Ryder's arm tightly around Ashley's shoulders, they reentered the kitchen, where Lucy and Pappy had apparently remained glued to their chairs.

"Howdy," Pappy greeted them. "Want some more orange juice?"

"Sure," Ryder said. "If you two are ever looking for Ashley, she'll be at my place."

"Oh-h-h," Ashley said, burying her face in her hands. "I'm not going to survive this man."

Ryder frowned. "Now what did I do wrong?"

"You're just so blunt, brother dear," Lucy said. "It's all right, Ashley, we're all family here. Honestly, Ryder, you are so dumb sometimes."

"All I said was—"

"They *know* what you said!" Ashley interrupted. "Oh, well, what the heck."

"Refuse to pick up his socks," Lucy said. "Just leave them on the floor until they rot."

"Got it." Ashley nodded.

Ryder scowled, and began to rummage through the kitchen cupboards, making a great deal of noise as he did so.

"What are you looking for?" Lucy asked.

"Extra frying pans. Ashley burns one a meal and it's going to cost me a fortune."

Pappy cackled merrily, then got up and kissed Ashley on the cheek.

"Patience, missy," he said, then went out the back door.

The afternoon passed quickly and pleasantly. Maria and John, a quiet couple in their fifties, returned from church, and Maria prepared a huge lunch for everyone. Every time Ashley looked up, Maria smiled at her, then at Ryder, then at Ashley again, until Lucy dissolved in a fit of laughter. Later, Ryder hitched a horse to a small wagon and gave Ashley a tour of the ranch. They laughed and talked, smiled a great deal, and shared an endless number of lengthy kisses. When Ryder said it was time to return to town, Ashley grabbed Lucy and dashed to the barn for one last look at the kittens.

"Little girls and kittens," Pappy said with humor to Ryder.

"Maybe when they're old enough," Ryder said, "I'll surprise her with one, if she's still—" He cut himself off.

"Still with you?" Pappy finished for him. "Is that gnawin' at you, boy?"

"Can you blame me for wondering?"

"It was all a long time ago. Lucy's learnin' to put her grief behind her. Time you did too."

"It's different with me, Pappy. Accepting death is one thing, but . . ."

"Do you love Ashley?"

"Yeah. Yeah, I do."

"And you'll never tell her. You'll leave her to stare into the night, with you right next to her in that bed, and she'll be achin' to hear the words. Where are you goin' to find enough room for love in your heart and soul, when you're so chocked full of anger and hurt?"

"Lighten up, Pappy. That's enough."

"Think about it, boy. And, Ryder?"

"Yeah?"

"See the doc tomorrow about your shoulder."

"Yeah."

Ashley came running into the room with her hair flying about her like an ebony cloud and her eyes sparkling with excitement.

"The kittens are so-o-o cute!" she said, circling Ryder's waist with her arms and smiling up at him. "I adore the black one with the white ears."

Ryder brushed her hair away from her face and smiled down at her tenderly. Oh, yes, he thought, he did love this woman. That love brought a warm glow to his heart and a knot of fear to his stomach at the same time. She was so small, so fragile, yet she had the power to destroy him. But then, she might also have the key to bringing him immeasurable joy. He just didn't know what the future held.

"*Now* can we go?" he asked, chuckling.

"Will we come again soon?"

"Yes, I promise."

"Well, then." She laughed. "I guess we can go."

"Home," Ryder said softly.

"Yes, Ryder. Home."

Pappy simply nodded, a smile on his weather-beaten face.

"You wore me out, Ashley," Lucy gasped, coming into the room. "I can't move that fast anymore."

"Strange things happened to her when she turned thirty," Ryder said. "Good-bye, old lady," he added, kissing Lucy on the cheek. "Remember, slow and easy, okay?"

"Don't worry, Ryder. I'm going to be just fine."

Good-byes were said, hugs exchanged, and Ashley and Ryder headed back to Houston.

"We'll go by the warehouse and collect your things," Ryder said.

"I should leave a note for Josh, letting him know where I've gone. Wrong. I don't need World War III on my hands."

"Tell him. I doubt if he's dumb enough to come pounding on my door."

"True. He says you have a very fast punch."

"I've had a lot of practice."

"Oh?"

"Do you have some empty boxes to pack your things in?"

"Yes." He'd slammed the door on her again, she thought. Where and why had he used his fists so much? She had to learn not to allow his silences to hurt her. She just had to.

Except for her furniture, all of Ashley's worldly goods were loaded into the back of the truck. When Ryder remarked on how little she had, she simply shrugged and said that military kids learn early not to be "savers." She insisted on driving her van to his apartment, silently daring him to comment on the aged vehicle's worthiness. He wisely said nothing. At the apartment Ryder made room for her in the dresser, closet, and medicine cabinet. Ashley waited for guilt to sweep over her as she placed her things next to his. She was actually moving in with this man! Twenty-five years of Victorian principles had been tossed out the window in a few short hours because of a tall Texan with emerald eyes. But the guilt did not come. She felt only an inner peace and contentment. She was home.

It wasn't the fairy tale of perfection she had fantasized about. Ryder didn't love her, refused to share his inner self, but there was nowhere else on earth she wished to be except by his side.

After dinner, Ashley spread the newspaper out on the floor, holding her heavy hair out of the way with one hand as she leaned over the small print.

"What are you doing?" Ryder asked, sinking onto the sofa and lighting a cigarette. "You have a cute tush," he added, reaching over and giving it a pat.

"I'm looking for a job."

"There's no rush on that."

"Being unemployed does not pay the rent."

"You don't have any rent to pay."

Ashley turned around and sat down, crossing her legs Indian style.

"I intend to put in my share, Ryder," she said.

"I'm not taking your money, Ashley. Why do I get the feeling we're about to have another wingding of an argument? And don't say something idiotic about your not being a kept woman or whatever."

"Well, I want to split expenses down the middle."

"Yep, here we go. This one is going to be a beaut."

"I don't want to fight with you, Ryder."

"Good. Then the subject is closed."

"It is not!"

"You're driving me nuts again!" he said, his voice rising.

"Don't you start hollering at me, Ryder Cantrell!"

"Oh, man." He stared up at the ceiling.

"Let's compromise."

"How?"

"I have no idea," she said, bursting into laughter. "I really don't."

"Come up here," he said, extending his hand to her.

"I have to find a job," she said, snuggling next to him. "I'll be bored out of my mind sitting around all day."

"I'll hire you. Can you pour concrete, lay bricks?"

"Nope."

"So much for that. Listen, you worked damn hard at that warehouse. Relax awhile before you go hustling out looking for something. Or go down to the office and mess around helping Lucy. She's always complaining that she's overworked."

"I'd just be in her way."

"No, you wouldn't. The point is, you're in a position to find exactly the kind of job you want. Don't grab the first one that comes along."

"That sounds reasonable."

"Good Lord, she agreed with me! Somebody write that down."

She laughed. "Oh, stop. You'll make out that we're incompatible."

"No way," he said, lifting her onto his lap. "We are very, *very* compatible."

As Ryder bent his head to claim her mouth, Ashley wound her arms about his neck, inching her fingers into his thick hair. His hand found the buttons on her blouse and freed them, then cupped her breast in his palm.

"I want you," he said, trailing his lips down her neck.

"Yes," she whispered. The heat from Ryder's thighs seemed to have set fire to a trail of passion throughout her entire body. She could feel his arousal straining against her, and ached for the fulfillment it would bring her. "Ryder, make love to me," she said. "Please."

With a throaty moan he lifted her into his arms and carried her into the bedroom. Clothes seemed to float away and they reached for each other, eager, ready, wanting to give and to receive. It was a celebration, a symphony of soaring violins. Ecstasy. When they were satiated, a delicious drowsiness settled over them and they slept.

The next thing to penetrate Ashley's consciousness was Ryder yelling, "Dammit to hell!" She sat bolt upright in the dark room and blinked against the fogginess of sleep.

"Ryder?" she said, as she realized he wasn't in the bed.

"I'm sorry. I'm trying to get dressed in the dark so I won't wake you."

She glanced at the clock. "It's only five."

"I have to be on the site. I got through my shower all right, but guess what I had taken in there to put on?"

"What?" she asked, switching on the light.

"These!" he yelled, waving a filmy bra and a lacy pair of bikini panties in the air.

"Oh, my." She burst into laughter. "You did give me that drawer, you know."

"Well, I forgot," he growled, rummaging through another drawer.

"You have a magnificent body," she said, her gaze flickering over his naked, muscular form.

"Like it, huh?" He chuckled. "Ah, here we go. Underwear. What every man needs."

"I'll make you some breakfast."

"No, go back to sleep. You're not the maid here, and there's no reason for you to be up so early."

"Talked me into it." She flopped back against the pillow and shut her eyes.

"Ashley?" Ryder said a short time later.

"Hmmm?"

"I've got to go. I'll see you later."

"Have a good day," she said, opening one eye.

"What are you going to do?"

"Don't know." She yawned.

"You're a real ball of fire there, kid."

"Sleepy."

"Kiss me."

"Absolutely."

After a kiss that made her tingle right down to her toes, Ashley burrowed into her pillow and went back to sleep. Ryder stood by the bed for a long moment and stared down at her. He was smiling when he strode from the room.

In Dr. Metcalf's office a few hours later, Ryder shrugged into his western shirt and began to snap it shut.

"Well?" he said. "What's the verdict?"

"It's what I was afraid of the last time you were in," Dr. Metcalf said. "You constantly use and develop those arm and shoulder muscles, and the scar tissue is becoming entwined with some nerves. I told you to take it easy."

"I have a living to make."

"You're in a lot of pain. I know you are, so don't try to deny it."

"I'll just have to get used to it, doc."

"Not this time," the doctor said. "Listen to me. I have to go in and get that scar tissue out of there before it's too late. If we wait, there's too big a risk of those nerves being damaged. It has to be done."

"Not now, doc," Ryder said, raking his hand through his hair.

"Yes, Ryder, now!"

"You don't understand," Ryder said, beginning to pace the floor. "The timing is lousy. I've got a special lady who's important to me. And there's Lucy to think of. She's just coming out of her shell. If I land in the hospital now, it will force her to relive everything about Jimmy again. I don't know if she could handle it."

"Ryder, this woman in your life and your sister are going to have to toughen up. You're the important party here. For once in your life think of yourself. Hell, man, do you want to lose the use of that arm? How are you going to make love to your woman then, hotshot?"

"Did they make you and Pappy out of the same mold?" Ryder said gruffly. "You two are hell to deal with."

"We're just good ole boys. You check into Methodist Hospital by eight tonight. I'm cutting your carcass at seven tomorrow morning."

"The hell you are!"

"I scheduled it as soon as I saw the X rays. Don't fight me on this, Ryder, because you're the only one who will lose."

"Damn."

"I agree. The accident was two years ago and I'm still patching you up. Well, get out of here. I'll see you tonight when I make my rounds."

"Yeah."

"I'm sorry, Ryder. I wish it were different. This woman you care for, Pappy, Lucy, they'd all agree that it would be damn foolish to wait."

"How long will I be laid up?"

"Hard to tell. A few weeks, maybe longer."

"Ashley comes into my life and I turn into an invalid. Wonderful."

"See you tonight."

"I can hardly wait." Ryder growled.

In a restaurant across town, Ashley and Lucy were just finishing lunch. They had chatted about clothes, movies, books, but not men.

"Lucy," Ashley said finally, "who is Pappy?"

"Ryder hasn't told you," Lucy said. "I was so wishing he had. He's changed, different, since he met you, Ashley, and it's wonderful. But there's so much churning inside of him. Maybe in time, with you, he'll open up. I just don't know."

"He won't let me close to him, Lucy. He starts to say something about Pappy, or makes a reference to when he was young, and then he closes the door. I want to really know him, understand who he is."

"You're in love with him, aren't you?" Lucy asked gently.

"Yes. Yes, I am."

"He's my brother and I love him with my whole heart, but, Ashley, he might hurt you so badly. He may never unlock those hidden chambers. Could you really be happy living that way?"

"I'm trying, I really am, but it hurts when he shuts me out."

"Of course it does, and rightly so. I'm sorry, but I can't tell you about Pappy and the nightmare Ryder carries inside of himself. I just can't, and neither can Pappy. It will be up to Ryder. It's his demon. When I talked to you about the accident, about Jimmy, I rid myself of my ghosts. Let's pray that Ryder tells you about his. But, Ashley, it's been so many years for him. Years of bitter memories. He may never be free. You may have to face that fact."

"I love him very much."

"I know, but sometimes even love isn't enough. I hope it works out for you two. I've dreamed about someone like you coming into Ryder's life, making him laugh and be happy. Now you're here and I'm grateful. The future, however, is a hazy blur. By the way, did he say anything to you about going to the doctor?"

"No."

"And he hasn't even phoned in to the office, that rat. Well, I'm going to track him down and pin him to the wall. Come on, there's safety in numbers."

"Well, in that case," Ashley said, "let's go find six or seven Marines and bring them along. *Big* Marines."

When the two women entered the office of Cantrell Construction, Ryder was sitting behind Lucy's desk, replacing the telephone receiver.

"I just called you," he said to Ashley. "You're not home."

"Very good." She smiled. "You figured that out all by yourself. Did you want to tell me something important?"

"Yeah, sort of."

"Take her into your office and kiss her, or whatever," Lucy ordered. "Get out of my chair."

"You might as well come, too, Lucy." Ryder got to

his feet. "No use hashing it over more than necessary."

"What's wrong?" Ashley asked, a knot tightening in her stomach, but Ryder had already started down the hall.

Ashley and Lucy exchanged glances and quickly followed Ryder into his office. He shoved his hands into the back pockets of his jeans and looked at their anxious faces, then let out a deep breath and shook his head.

"No use beating around the bush," he said. "I saw Doc Metcalf, and he . . . Well, he said . . ."

"Ryder, please," Ashley said.

"I have to have a little repair work done on my shoulder, that's all."

"Little? How little?" Lucy asked.

"The . . . uh . . . scar tissue is causing some problems, and the doc is going to get it out of there."

"You're going to have an operation?" Ashley asked, sinking onto a chair.

"Yeah."

"When?"

"Tomorrow morning. I'm checking into the hospital tonight. Hey, it's no big deal, more of an inconvenience than anything else."

"I don't believe that," Lucy said. "You'd have talked Dr. Metcalf into postponing it if it weren't imperative that it be done now. You've been in a lot of pain, Ryder. Ashley and I deserve to know the truth."

"Ryder?" Ashley's voice was soft.

"Dammit," he said, raking his hand through his hair, "I told the doc the timing was lousy. I don't want this in our lives, Ashley, not now. We're new, fragile. We don't need this crap. And what about you, Lucy? You've just begun to live again, and this is going to bring back all the memories about Jimmy and—"

"You just hold it!" Ashley said, jumping to her

feet. Ryder's eyes widened in surprise. "Who appointed you everyone's guardian angel? The important person here is you. I'm not going to fall apart, and neither is Lucy. We're women, not little girls, and you are not our baby-sitter. Facts, Ryder, and now! Why the rush to have the surgery?"

"If I wait, the nerves will be further damaged and I could . . . lose the use of my arm." A muscle tightened in his jaw.

"Dear Lord," Lucy whispered.

"Well, then," Ashley said, her voice trembling, "you have no choice, do you? Do you own any pajamas?"

"Huh?"

"You must have new pajamas. People always get new pajamas when they go to the hospital. It's an American tradition for someone to . . . Ryder, would you hold me for just a minute if I promised not to cry?"

"Ah, babe," he said, closing the distance between them and pulling her into his arms. "I'm so sorry about this."

"Don't say that." She spoke into his shirt front. "It's not your fault, and you mustn't worry about me and Lucy."

"Let's see." Lucy tapped her chin with her fingertip. "Can we use the sports car while you're in the hospital? Ashley and I are going to scout the bars. Oops, my phone is ringing." She hurried from the room.

"Ashley," Ryder asked, "are you really all right?"

"I hate everything about this, Ryder, but that's fair, I think. Wishing isn't going to make it go away, so we'll just face it head-on and get through it. Together. Together, Ryder. That's the key word here."

"You are incredible, my lady," he said, tilting her

chin up. His kiss was long and powerful, and left her trembling.

"We're all going to be fine," she said breathlessly. "Me, Lucy, Pappy, all of us. You've got to concentrate on yourself and do everything that the doctors tell you."

"And the nurses?" He grinned at her.

"Only grandmotherly types will be allowed on your case."

"Got it. I wish I could spend the afternoon with you, but I have so many loose ends to take care of. Would you like to go out to dinner? I don't have to be at the hospital until eight."

"Would you mind if we just stayed home? I don't want to share you with anyone."

"Sounds good to me. I'd better call Pappy and fill him in. Listen, I have a very important assignment for you."

"Really? What is it?"

"Go buy me some pajamas!"

Seven

After another intoxicating kiss, Ashley left Ryder's office. "Lucy," she said, stopping at the desk, "are you all right?"

"I won't let Ryder down." Lucy managed a weak smile. "I promise. How are you?"

"Off to buy pajamas for my master." She waved breezily.

Once safely inside the empty elevator, Ashley leaned against the wall and drew a shaky breath. The thought of Ryder having surgery, lying in pain in a stark hospital room, brought an icy wave of fear and misery washing over her. It wasn't fair! she cried silently. The accident had been two years ago, and it was still a living nightmare. No, she would *not* panic. Ryder was big, strong, and healthy, and would come through this thing just fine. He would. He just had to!

She bought Ryder royal-blue pajamas, then, on impulse, drove to her warehouse. She entered the empty building and wandered slowly through it, listening to her echoing footsteps and the sound of the beating of her own heart.

So much had changed in her life so rapidly, and had created such tempestuous emotions. Her hopes and dreams in the form of Plants-to-Go had been shattered simply by the arrival of a letter—a letter that had brought her storming into Ryder Cantrell's life. And he had staked a claim on her heart forever. And now he was to have an operation, one that she knew would bring back vivid and painful memories of that horrifying day two years ago.

"Oh, damn," she said, brushing a tear from her cheek. "I hate this. I really, really hate this." Well, okay, she thought, so it was crummy, but there was nothing she could do about it. She'd conduct herself with decorum and dignity. "And buy him a new coloring book and crayons. Oh, hell."

Ashley stomped out of the warehouse and climbed behind the wheel of the van. Her next stop was at a market, where she bought huge steaks, fresh broccoli, and a loaf of crusty French bread. She was going to prepare a delicious meal for Ryder, so he could at least remember what good food tasted like, while he was in the hospital.

When she returned to the apartment, she showered and shampooed her hair, brushing it into a glowing cascade down her back as she used the blow dryer. She dressed in white slacks and a gauzy pink blouse, then set the table for two. The sound of Ryder's key in the door brought her rushing from the kitchen and into his arms. His greeting was a passionate kiss that left her smiling.

"Hello, pretty lady," he said when he lifted his head. "You smell good, taste good, feel good. You, in short, are nice to come home to."

"Thank you. I'm glad I'm here. I've got a lovely dinner planned for us."

"I'll go shower. And, Ashley? I really am sorry about this mess."

"Don't apologize. You act as though you have a choice. Did you talk to Pappy?"

"Yeah, I told him what was going on. He just said to quit belly-achin' and get the thing over with."

"My sentiments exactly," Ashley said. "Go take a shower."

"Lord," Ryder muttered, striding from the room.

"I love you, Ryder," Ashley whispered, then turned and walked slowly to the kitchen. So far, so good, she thought. She was worried, needless to say, but relatively calm. Ryder would be fine, but, oh, goodness, she'd be so glad when the whole thing was over with! Those doctors had better know what they were doing! "Smile," she told herself firmly.

Ryder reappeared, dressed in jeans and a gray shirt. His hair was damp from his shower, and he smelled soapy and fresh as he nuzzled Ashley's neck.

"Don't nibble on the cook," she said, poking him in the ribs.

"Or what? You'll burn the frying pan?"

"Yep."

"I'll buy you a truckload of frying pans. Your hair smells so good, all lemony."

"Unhand me, villain. I'm working here."

Ryder leaned against the counter and crossed his arms over his broad chest as he watched Ashley move around the kitchen.

"You look so right here," he said quietly. "I don't mean because you're cooking my meal. I mean here, in my home. I'll be back as soon as I can. I'll raise a bunch of hell and they'll be glad to let me out of the hospital. Thing is, while I'm away I want you to stay out at the ranch."

"Ryder, no," Ashley said, stopping in the middle of the room. "I want to be close to the hospital so I can see you as often as they'll let me."

"No. I want to know you're there with Pappy and Lucy. Pappy will drive you out tonight. He's meeting us at the hospital with Lucy, so she can drive my truck back."

"We could have discussed it, you know," Ashley said, a frown on her face.

"No time." He grinned. "We might have argued right up to the minute I have to leave, and I intend to use those hours making sweet, slow love to my lady. Now, tell me, darlin', doesn't that sound much better than hollering about something that I intend to have my way about anyway?"

Ashley opened her mouth to protest, but instead, a bubble of laughter escaped from her lips.

"You're spoiled rotten, Cantrell. You're stubborn and arrogant and rotten."

"True, but I'm lovable."

Oh, yes, she thought, very, very lovable. "Well," she said, "since it will mean I can see my kitten, I'll agree to your plan."

Ryder laughed, and reached out his long arms to pull her into his embrace.

"You are something," he said, his green eyes sparkling. "You're a handful, Ashley Hunt. Just remember, my hands are the only ones you fill."

"How profound," she sniffed. "Say, did you agree to loan Lucy and me the sports car?"

"No!"

"Oh, pooh."

"Hell, there I'd be flat on my back, and I'd have to come bail you two out of jail."

"Have you no faith?"

"What I have is some smarts."

"Stingy," she said, wiggling out of his arms. "Add that to the list. Let's eat."

Their lighthearted mood prevailed through the meal, but when Ryder leaned back in his chair and lit a cigarette, the tension began to creep in around them. Ashley felt it churn in her stomach as she gazed across the table at Ryder. He was so big and strong, like a warrior. His skin was as bronzed as if he were a statue, and his body was perfectly proportioned. The green of his eyes changed with his mood, and his smooth gait was as graceful and powerful as a panther's. He was Ryder. And she loved him.

And she didn't want him to go to the hospital. She knew he had to have the surgery, but at that moment she just wanted to put her arms around him and pull him close, refuse to let him go. No, she told herself. Facts were facts, and Ryder was going to have the operation. But, oh, dammit!

"Ashley, don't," Ryder said quietly. "You're a breath away from crying, and it won't help."

"I'm sorry. I promised myself I wouldn't fall apart, and I won't. It's just that—"

"I know." He covered her hand with his. "I've turned this around in my mind and I realize that if it were you going into that hospital tonight I'd be crazy with worry and anger. I'd probably end up decking someone just to try and feel better. Maybe you *should* cry. It's a nice privilege of your gender. Me, I'd hit somebody."

"No, tears won't solve anything. Besides, my nose gets all red when I cry." She took a deep breath. "You should go pack. I'll clean up this mess."

"You need to pack too."

"I will. You go ahead."

Ryder nodded and pushed himself to his feet, gazing at her for a long moment before turning and leaving the room. Ashley cleaned the kitchen, issuing herself firm directives as she went about her chores. Smile. No tears. She would give Ryder no reason to worry about her, would leave him free to concentrate on what he was facing, knowing she was capable of doing her part. Smile.

Ryder pulled a small suitcase out of the closet and set it on the bed. He tossed in the pajamas Ashley had purchased, then stood perfectly still. He felt as though the weight of the world were resting on his back, leaving him exhausted, hardly able to move. Everything was closing in on him, crushing him. He was angry, frustrated, and scared to death. The fear was not for the operation, the pain it would bring. The fear was that he was about to lose everything he had.

Everything? he asked himself. No, that wasn't even close to rational. Lucy, Pappy, Cantrell Construction, the ranch, they would be there when this was over. Lucy was hanging in there, determined not to fall prey to the horrifying memories of the past, of Jimmy. No, the knot in his gut was caused by one woman. Ashley.

Before they had even been given a chance, he was going to fail her. His promise of strength and protection was being ripped away from him. He would be less than he had declared himself to be, and therefore would not be good enough.

Memories of the years of struggling to be the best in the eyes of those who continually passed judgment on him came rushing back. Then he had been Ryder the misfit, the rebel, the outcast. The one who fought with his fists and built a wall around his heart. Until now. Until Ashley.

Lord, how he loved her. He sure as hell hadn't intended to. It had just happened. And now she had the power to destroy him. She would see him weak and needing care, see that he couldn't fulfill his promise, find him lacking, and . . . then leave him. Like those before, she would cast him aside, and he would have no defense against the hurt it would bring.

Loving Ashley was a mistake.

And Ryder Cantrell did *not* like to make mistakes.

With a tight set to his jaw, Ryder finished packing and placed the suitcase by the door. Then he stretched out on the bed and laced his fingers behind his head.

"Ryder?" Ashley said softly from the doorway .

"Yeah?"

"Are you okay?"

He shifted to rest on his elbows and gazed at Ashley. The soft glow from the lamp seemed to cast a halo around her ebony hair. She appeared so young, so frightened, as she ran her tongue nervously across her bottom lip.

Ah, hell, Ryder thought. She was so lovely. He loved this woman so much, and for now, for this moment, that was all that mattered. The tomorrows would just have to wait.

"Ryder?"

"Let me make love to you, Ashley," he said, his voice husky.

A gentle smile came onto her face as she walked slowly to the side of the bed. Ryder held out his hand to her, but she stepped back just beyond his reach.

"What . . ." he began; then his breath caught in his throat as he realized her intention.

With steady hands she undid the buttons on her gauzy blouse and quickly shed the garment. Her bra followed close behind, revealing her ivory breasts to Ryder's smoldering view. As she drew her slacks and panties down her slender legs, he could feel the blood pounding in his veins, his manhood stirring against his tight jeans.

Her hair fell forward as she bent over to pull off her shoes, then she stood naked before him with an expression of serenity on her face.

Ryder was unable to speak as their eyes met in a timeless gaze. He had heard her unspoken plea when he had given her his shirt to cover herself, and now she was whispering a message that she had even greater trust in him to cherish what she offered. He was shaken not only physically by the vision before him, but emotionally as well. She had grown so much, come so far . . . for him.

"Ashley," he said, his voice hushed, "for you to stand before me as you are now is a memory I will always treasure. Thank you, my lady."

"I *am* yours, Ryder," she answered, walking to the bed. "I am."

He pushed himself to his feet and cupped her face in his hands, kissing her with a restraint that caused his muscles to tremble. Drawing a steadying breath, he moved away to shed his clothing as Ashley swept back the blankets and then turned to face him. Inches apart, they didn't touch, and their desires soared with anticipation.

"Love me, Ryder." Ashley's voice was so soft, he could hardly hear her.

"Oh, yes," he replied, "but I want you so badly, I'll rush you. Give me a minute to . . ."

"To what?" she asked, boldly running her hands over the mass of curly hair on his chest.

"Ashley!" he said gruffly, pushing her back onto the bed and covering her body with his.

Their mouths met, lips parted, tongues dueled, and passions flared. Softness molded to hardness. Hands and lips blazed molten paths over each other as their breathing became labored and heartbeats quickened.

"Now, Ryder," Ashley gasped.

Ryder clenched his teeth as he strove for control, then quickly prepared himself. He claimed her mouth again in a searing kiss and at last, *at last,* moved over her and entered her honeyed warmth with a bold thrust of his manhood.

Ashley rose to meet him, to fill herself with him, with his strength and power. Deeper and deeper within her he moved, and she matched his rhythm. They crested the crashing waves of ecstasy together, calling to each other. In shuddering spasms they rode out the storm, then clung together as they slowly drifted back to a place of reason and reality.

"Oh, Ashley," Ryder said with a moan, burying his face in the sweet fragrance of her hair.

"So beautiful," she said.

He lifted his weight from her and pulled her close, nestling her to his chest as he gently stroked her hair.

"Oh, Ashley," he said again.

Never had her name been spoken with such reverence, she thought, and held fast to the memory.

Time passed and they lay still, cloaked in contentment, hearts beating in steady rhythms, hands resting lightly on each other.

"I have to go," Ryder said finally.

"So soon?"

"I'm going to be late as it is, and Doc Metcalf will jump my butt. He'll probably take ten extra blood tests, or something, to let me know who's boss. I swear, they did not make hospital beds for tall people. I'll be a pretzel by the time I get out of there. The food stinks, too."

Ashley smiled. "Anything else?"

"I'm practicing my complaining so they won't

want me around. Come to think of it, though, I wonder if that blond nurse is still— Ow!" he yelled as Ashley tugged a tawny curl on his chest. "Gently there, woman. Lord, they're going to shave my chest. Do you have any idea how much that itches when it grows back? It drives me nuts! And then there's those damn sponge baths. Demeaning, that's what. And Jell-O. I hate Jell-O. I'm not going. Nope, I refuse."

"Good. Cancel the whole silly business."

"I've got to get going," he said, kissing her on the forehead and swinging off the bed. "I'll take a quick shower. It's the last one I'll get for a while."

Ashley watched as Ryder closed the bathroom door behind him, her heart nearly bursting with love. She knew he was striving to lighten the mood, bring a touch of humor to the situation, for her. He was thinking of her and her needs, trying to make her smile. And she loved him for it. And for the exquisite beauty they had shared in their joining. And for just being himself.

With a sigh, Ashley buried her face in Ryder's pillow, drinking in his special aroma. Finally, she roused herself and pulled on her clothes. She packed a few things in her suitcase, braided her hair into a single plait, then walked into the living room.

"Ready?" Ryder asked, joining her a few minutes later.

"Yes."

Dressed in his jeans and western shirt, he appeared massive and strong, and she melted against him when he pulled her into his arms.

"Ashley," he said, his voice strained, "be here when I come home."

"Yes, of course."

"Just say it, okay? Tell me you'll be here."

"I'll be waiting for you, Ryder," she said, confused

by the urgency in his voice, its slightly frantic quality. "You know that."

"No, I . . . Yeah, okay."

"Ryder, I *will* be here."

But for how long? he wondered. Dammit, for how long? He kissed her, almost roughly, then gruffly said, "Let's go."

In the garage, Ashley hesitated.

"Wouldn't it be easier if I had my van?" she asked.

"No, I want you with me," he said, leading her to the sports car.

"Oh, great. I'll drive."

"Ha!"

"Well, darn."

The drive to the hospital was sprinkled with light conversation. When they entered the brightly lit building, Ryder circled Ashley's shoulders with his arm and pulled her close to his side.

"Ah, hell," he muttered, "the troops have gathered to pounce."

"You're late," Dr. Metcalf said.

"Yeah, I know," Ryder said, frowning. "Hello, Lucy, Pappy."

"Hi, sweetheart," Lucy said, kissing him on the cheek.

"How are you doing?"

"I'm fine, Ryder. Really."

"Take care of my ladies, Pappy."

"You bet, boy. You just get yourself patched up."

"Yeah, well, tell that to your knife-happy friend, here."

"Piece of cake," Dr. Metcalf said. "Move your butt, Ryder. You've got papers to fill out and I have tests to run on your worthless carcass."

Ryder set his suitcase on the floor and hugged

Lucy tightly, then with no hesitation did the same to Pappy.

"Two seconds," Ryder said, taking Ashley's hand and leading her to a corner.

"Kiss her quick," the doctor ordered.

"That man is cold," Ryder muttered. "Ashley, I'll see you tomorrow. There is nothing at all to worry about. Doc is the best."

"All right."

"See you soon, babe." He cupped her face in his hands and placed a fleeting kiss on her lips .

And then he was gone.

Ashley watched him go, seeing the wide, straight set to his shoulders, the easy, loping gait, the man she loved.

"Time to go, missy," Pappy said, coming over to her.

"But—"

"Come on, darlin'. They won't let you see him anymore tonight. Lucy and I will drive back in the truck. You use the sports car."

"Me?"

"Ryder told me you're to use it for comin' back and forth."

"Oh, dear me. What if I dent a fender or something?"

"That boy doesn't place that much importance on a fancy car. He just didn't want you in that van of yours. You follow us, so you don't get lost."

"I'll ride with her, Pappy," Lucy said.

"Fine, then."

"Pappy," Ashley said, "will we be able to see Ryder in the morning before his surgery?"

"Nope. He'll be all drugged up. We'll come in early and wait until it's over."

"Yes. Wait," she repeated, glancing once more

down the hall where Ryder had gone. "I love him, Pappy."

"I know, missy. I'm old, but I'm not a fool. I know you love my boy, and I'm mighty glad you do. Let's go home."

By the time they were halfway to the ranch, Lucy was laughing uproariously.

"You drive like a wild woman!" she gasped, hanging on to her seat.

"It's not my fault! I'm hardly touching the gas pedal and it goes crazy. Oh, why did Ryder do this to me?"

"I guess he thought you'd be safer than in your van. Little did he know you're a menace on the road." Lucy giggled again. "This is so funny, I can't stand it."

"Then *you* drive the stupid car!"

"No way. Ryder didn't give me permission. It's all yours."

"Thanks a bunch."

Ashley was still sputtering when they entered the ranch house, and vowed never again to drive that awful vehicle. Pappy poured glasses of his famous orange juice, and the three sat at the kitchen table. A silence fell upon them until Pappy finally stood up.

"I think I'll turn in," he said. "We've got a long day ahead tomorrow. We'd best eat breakfast 'bout six and head into town."

"All right, Pappy," Lucy agreed.

"Good night, Pappy," Ashley said.

"Don't stay up late," he said, and left the room.

"So far," Lucy said, "you and I are doing fairly well, don't you think?"

"I'm hanging on by a thread, Lucy."

"You were great at the hospital."

"Did the doctor say how long the surgery will take?"

"It will be about four hours."

"Oh, God," Ashley whispered.

"Don't start thinking about it. Pappy's right, we have a big day tomorrow. I'll show you to your room and you can get some rest. I've had it too. I just hope I can sleep."

The bedroom where Ashley was to stay was decorated in a combination of Indian and Spanish motifs and was alive with vibrant colors. After a quick shower, she pulled on her nightie and slipped between the sheets, staring up into the darkness. Ryder's face danced before her eyes with such clarity she felt as though she could reach out and touch him.

"Sleep well, my love," she said softly. "And I *will* be here when you come home. I heard the shout of your whispers, and I *will* be here." What had brought that near-desperate edge to Ryder's voice when he had needed to hear her say those words aloud? she mused. She wouldn't think about it tonight. She had to sleep and get ready to face tomorrow.

When the alarm went off, Ashley hushed the shrill sound and foggily wondered where she was. When the realization hit her, she hurried from the bed and dressed in blue slacks and a pale blue blouse, then brushed her hair until it shone. She would wear it loose, the way Ryder liked it.

Breakfast was quiet. Maria prepared it, and although Ashley, Lucy, and Pappy ate, they hardly tasted their food. Pappy drove to the hospital in his truck, and Ashley and Lucy followed him in Ryder's car. Ashley was getting the hang of driving the fast sports car, and thought that under different circumstances she might actually enjoy it. When they reached the hospital, they were directed to the surgical waiting room.

"Ryder has the easy part," Pappy remarked. "He gets to sleep through the whole thing while we sit here stewin'. Lord knows, though, I'd change places with him if I could."

"I know you would, Pappy," Lucy said. "There's nothing to worry about. Ryder is healthy as a horse, and Dr. Metcalf is an excellent surgeon. Ryder will be fine."

"Who are you convincin'?" Pappy asked.

"Me," Lucy replied. "I'm scared out of my mind. Tell me to shut up. Ashley, you're white as a ghost."

"I'm okay. I just wish I could have seen him this morning, that's all. I really am all right."

And so it began.

The wait.

They chatted, then fell silent, then talked again. They paced the floor, drank endless cups of coffee, and flipped through magazines without actually seeing them. The clock on the wall moved with agonizing slowness and the morning dragged by. When four hours had passed with no sign of Dr. Metcalf, Ashley was no longer able to sit in her chair. She leaned against the wall . . . and waited.

It had been nearly five hours when Dr. Metcalf appeared.

"Festive-looking group," he said with a broad smile. "Now, before you all jump on me at once, Ryder is fine. He's in the recovery room, sleeping like a baby. The operation took longer than expected, since there was more scar tissue in there than showed on the X rays, but I did a fantastic job, if I do say so myself."

"When can we see him?" Lucy asked.

"He'll be in his room in a half hour or so, but I expect he'll sleep until this evening. When he does wake up I'll knock him right back out, because he's going to be in a lot of pain. You're welcome to sit with him, but at this point he doesn't give a damn whether you're there or not."

"I'd still like to stay," Ashley said.

"Buy these pretty gals some lunch, Pappy," the doctor suggested. "I'll see you all later."

"It's over." Ashley pressed her hands to her cheeks.

"No, missy," Pappy said, chuckling, "it's just beginnin'. Now we got us a wounded bear on our hands."

"Oh, ugh," Lucy said. "I'm moving to Alaska."

Lunch was a hurried affair in the hospital cafeteria, and then they went to Ryder's room. As they entered, a nurse was adjusting the IV bottle that dripped steadily through a tube taped to Ryder's hand. Without realizing she had done so, Ashley gripped Pappy's arm. He patted her hand gently.

"He's snug as a bug," the nurse assured them. "Just don't expect him to carry on a conversation. I'll be back in a bit," she added, going out of the door.

"Oh, no!" Lucy exclaimed, backing away from the bed. "He looks so still, as though he's—"

"Lucy, Ryder is alive," Ashley said. "He's alive! You get a handle on yourself right now or go out that door."

"I'm sorry," Lucy said. "Oh, Ashley, I really am sorry."

"He sure is gift wrapped." Pappy peered at the enormous bandage covering Ryder's shoulder and half of his chest.

"He's beautiful," Ashley said.

"Well, no sense standin' here starin' at him," Pappy said. "We know he came through it fine and he's out cold. Might as well go on back to the ranch until after supper."

"I'd better go to the office," Lucy said.

"I'm staying right here," Ashley insisted. "Dr. Metcalf said it would be all right."

"There's really no point to it," Pappy said.

"Please, Pappy, I want to be with him."

"Sure thing, missy."

"Thank you," she said, hugging Pappy, then Lucy.

"I'll be sunshine itself when he wakes up," Lucy promised. "I'll be back later."

After Lucy and Pappy had gone, Ashley pulled a chair close to the bed and sat down. She was nearly eye level with the bandage on Ryder's shoulder, and she glanced at it quickly, then scrutinized his face.

Ryder's deep tan was startlingly dark against the stark white of the bandage and the hospital linen. His hair was tousled, and Ashley resisted the urge to brush it back from his forehead. His features were as relaxed as a sleeping child's. His chest rose and fell with his deep, easy breathing.

The worst was over, Ashley thought, the surgery completed. Now, surrounded by the people who loved him, Ryder would regain his strength, and time would heal his wounds until he was free at last from the pain. He would emerge tall and strong and whole again.

"I'm here, Ryder," she whispered. "For as long as you want me, I'm here."

The afternoon crept by, and Ryder did not stir. Dr. Metcalf stopped in, and declared everything to be fine.

Just after four o'clock, while a nurse was hooking up a fresh IV bottle, Ryder moaned softly and moved his head on the pillow. Ashley was instantly on her feet, and she gripped the railing at the edge of the bed.

"Damn," Ryder mumbled, but he did not open his eyes.

"I'll go get the doctor," the nurse said, and left the room.

"Ryder?" Ashley asked softly.

"Yeah?" He spoke groggily, his lashes lifting slowly to reveal cloudy green eyes.

"It's Ashley."

"So, Sleeping Beauty awakes," Dr. Metcalf said, bustling in the door. "How are you feeling, Ryder?"

"Damn."

"Sounds about right. Thirsty?"

"Yeah."

"Ashley, put an ice chip in his mouth from that container."

Ryder accepted the ice, but Ashley had the distinct impression he had looked at her as though he had never seen her before in his life.

"He's not all here yet," Dr. Metcalf explained, seeing Ashley's frown. "Come on, Ryder, snap out of it so I can knock you back out with some pain-killer."

"That's the craziest thing I've ever heard," Ashley said.

"Ah, hell." Ryder shifted slightly on the bed. "Who hit me?" he asked, his words slurred.

"I did." Dr. Metcalf leaned over and checked Ryder's eyes with a pencil flashlight, then took his pulse. "Believe it or not, you're going to live. I'm going to order something for the pain. I just needed to know you'd come out of the anesthesia all right before I put you under any deeper."

"No, no," Ryder said, moving his head restlessly on the pillow. "Don't want . . ."

"Tough. You're getting it. We went through this battle two years ago when you didn't want any drugs. I won then, and I'll win now."

"Damn."

"That boy has a limited vocabulary."

"Where's Ashley?"

"I'm here, Ryder."

"Where in the hell is Ashley? Oh-h-h," he moaned. "Damn."

"The party's over for now," Dr. Metcalf said. "I'll send the nurse in to shoot him in his pretty tush. See you later."

"Ryder, I really am here. It's Ashley."

"Yeah?"

"Yeah." She placed her hand gently on his cheek.

"Well, damn," he said, smiling very crookedly. "That's nice. Stay close, huh?"

"There's nowhere else I want to be."

"Oh, man, I've been hit by a train."

"The nurse will be here soon with something for the pain."

"I hate that junk. I don't like having anything take over my mind, my body."

"I know," she said softly. "You like being in control of things. Do you want some more ice?"

"No. Is everybody okay?"

"We're all fine. Don't worry about anyone but yourself. Lucy and Pappy will be back later to see you."

"Ashley?"

"Yes?"

"Ashley, I'm . . ." His voice trailed off as his eyes drifted closed. "I'm glad you're here."

Eight

Pain. Hot, searing pain.

Like a branding iron burning through flesh to bone.

Ryder struggled to open his eyes, but found the effort too great. His mind was a jumble of confusion, and he fought against a rush of panic as he tried desperately to move, to prove to himself that he was alive. But, he forced himself to think, if he were dead there would be no pain, so he wasn't dead. The agony proved it, and now he welcomed it.

Who hated him enough to torment him like this? he wondered. Jimmy. Jimmy was angry because he had let go of his wrist and forced him to die. Didn't Jimmy know how sorry he was? Hadn't he told him enough times in the dreams, night after night? Jimmy had to listen, be made to understand that he hadn't meant to lose his grip, but the cable had broken and . . .

"Jimmy, no!" Ryder moaned. "Jimmy!"

"Oh, God," Lucy whispered.

"Ryder," Pappy said, "wake up, boy. Come on, son, open your eyes. Put the dream away and say hello to Ashley. She's here, Ryder, waiting for you."

Ashley? he thought. No, that didn't make sense, because Ashley was now and Jimmy was then. Ashley was waiting for him? He'd asked her to do that because he loved her. He wanted to be in the now so he could see her. Jimmy must go back in his grave and leave him be, because Ashley was here.

"Ashley?" Ryder slowly opened his eyes.

"Yes." She placed her hand on his cheek.

"Okay," Ryder said, letting out a long breath. "Yeah, okay. Damn."

"You with us, boy?" Pappy asked.

"Yeah. Pappy, I want to see Metcalf."

"He'll be comin' around."

"Now, Pappy!"

"Easy, boy. I'll go find him."

"Ryder, what's wrong?" Ashley asked. "Is the pain worse? You slept a long time after that shot and it's probably wearing off. They'll give you another one, so that—"

"No! No more. Damn, they've got me wrapped up like a mummy. Where's Lucy?"

"I'm here. You've been hollering about everything already, Ryder."

"Are you okay, Lucy?"

"Yes, Ryder, I'm fine. You look like hell, though."

"Feel like it, too." He attempted to smile and failed. "What's for dinner?"

"Liquid whatever," Lucy said, glancing at the IV.

"Wonderful."

"All right, hotshot," Dr. Metcalf said, coming into the room with Pappy, "what's on your mind?"

"No more drugs, doc," Ryder said fiercely. "None."

"Ryder, we've been over this before."

"No more! Those shots take me straight into hell, and I'm not going again!"

"Ryder, I tore your shoulder apart and stitched it back together. The pain—"

"It's real! It's here, and I can handle it. Dammit, doc, don't do this to me."

"Oh, Ryder," Ashley said, fighting back tears, "don't do this to *yourself*. You don't have to suffer."

"Doc, are you hearing me?" Ryder asked, perspiration glistening on his face and chest.

"I hear you," he answered quietly. "All right, you win. I'll write the order on your chart. No pain shot unless you request it but, dammit, ask for one if it gets too bad."

"Yeah. Thanks, doc." Ryder took a deep breath. "I'm hungry."

"You're what?" Ashley said, her eyes wide. "You just put all of us through a horrendous day, you refuse to ease your pain so we can have the pleasure of watching you suffer, your shoulder is held together by string and a prayer, and you're hungry? You've got a helluva lot of nerve, Cantrell! How dare you be hungry! I can't believe I just said all that."

"Oh, man, isn't she cute?" Ryder grinned. "She is just adorable."

Dr. Metcalf laughed. "I'll order you a tray. Pappy, you've got your hands full with those two, not to mention Lucy. I'm getting out of this zoo."

"Can't blame you for that," Pappy said.

Ashley watched as Ryder closed his eyes and clenched his teeth. He was pale despite his tan, and his breathing was slightly labored. She blinked back her tears as she saw him fighting his pain. She wanted to beg him to accept the shot that would bring him relief. His mind was made up, though, and she knew it, but why was he doing this to himself?

Pappy touched Ashley's arm and she looked at him quickly, seeing the concern on his wrinkled face.

"Lucy," Pappy said, "it's time we were heading home. Ashley can come along later."

" 'Bye, Ryder." Lucy leaned over and kissed him on the cheek. "I'll see you tomorrow."

"Hang in there, Lucy," Ryder said.

" 'Night, son," Pappy said.

"Thanks for everything, Pappy."

Ashley sank onto the chair next to Ryder's bed, but before she could speak, an elderly, plump nurse came scurrying in the door.

"Howdy, handsome," she said to Ryder. "Orders are to remove your IV because you're going on the Jell-O circuit."

"Hell."

"Feel the same way about Jell-O myself. Let's get this contraption out of the way and give you one good arm at least to hold that pretty girl's hand."

As the nurse left the room, Ryder flexed his fingers, then extended his hand to Ashley. She moved around to the other side of the bed and held his hand between both of hers.

"Hello, my lady," he said quietly.

"Hello, my Ryder."

"Crawl in this bed with me. It's lonely in here."

"There's hardly room for you."

"I'll share."

"Ryder, I don't want to nag, but couldn't you compromise? At least have a small amount of pain-killer? Please, Ryder? It's so difficult to see you like this."

Ryder frowned and looked at Ashley's pale face, heard the slight trembling in her voice.

"Yeah, babe, okay. I'll tell the doc. Just enough to take the edge off but not knock me out. I'll do it, I promise."

"Thank you."

"Room service," a woman's voice said. "Finest cuisine in Houston."

"Like hell," Ryder muttered.

"Lord, you're gorgeous," the gray-haired woman remarked. "No wonder everyone is buzzing about you. The nurses are yakking about the shoulder surgery on this floor. There's a good-looking broken knee on two, but you've got him beat. Okay, Mr. Body, let's crank you up a bit, so you can really enjoy this junk. I'll do all the work. You just lay there and bat those long eyelashes at me."

"Do *you* want to crawl in this bed with me?" Ryder asked. "I just got turned down."

"I'm too much of a woman for you, honey. Up you go."

A few minutes later, Ryder was propped against the pillows, scowling at the tray before him. He looked like a pouting little boy, and Ashley burst into laughter.

"You said you were hungry, so eat," she said. "Chicken broth, rice pudding, and—ta-da—Jell-O!"

"Hell."

"Eat!"

"Okay!"

Ryder grumbled his way through the meal but ate everything on his tray, including the Jell-O, declaring himself to be desperate. He then leaned his head back against the pillows and closed his eyes. Ashley removed the tray and lowered the bed.

"You're exhausted," she said. "I'm going to go now."

"No, wait." He reached for her hand. "Just a few more minutes. I know I'm being selfish, because you've had a long day, but stay a little longer."

"All right." She sat down again.

"I've put you through a lot, haven't I?" he asked quietly.

"No. The good with the bad, that's how it works. All this will be over and then we'll go on with our lives."

"It's not that simple. I'm not going to walk out of here tomorrow as good as new."

"I realize that."

"Do you? Hell, Ashley, I can't even hold you in my arms, or make love to you, or . . ."

"You will. Later. I'll wait."

"Will you, Ashley? Will you?" He squeezed her hand so tightly, she winced.

"Ryder, I love you," she whispered.

"What?"

"Maybe this isn't the time to tell you, but maybe it is. I love you, Ryder Cantrell. With my whole heart, mind, soul, and body, I love you."

"You do?"

"Yes, I do."

"I'll be damned. That is . . . really something."

"You don't seem too thrilled."

"I'm just surprised. I mean, I . . . I'll be damned. I don't think you're too bright, Ashley."

"Well, thanks a whole helluva lot!"

"Why did you fall in love with a man who's carved up like a Thanksgiving turkey? That was dumb. Really dumb."

"Shut up, Cantrell. You make me so mad. What is this? A centerfold contest? Good grief, you're impossible. I don't care if they transplant an extra nose onto your face. I love you, the man, not the package you happen to come in."

"I—"

"I'm going to leave now and let you rest. I'll see you in the morning." She stood up and kissed him on the forehead. "I do love you. Good night."

" 'Night, babe," he said, watching as she left the room. Ashley loved him? he thought with wonder. She loved him? What exactly did that mean? For now, today, in a wave of pity, because he was flat on his back? How long would she love him? *How damn long?*

"Oh, man." Ryder flung his good arm over his eyes.

"What do you say we ease that pain just a bit, son?" Dr. Metcalf suggested from the doorway. "I won't put you under, I promise."

"Yeah, okay." Ryder sighed. "I'm tired. I'm just tired . . . of everything."

Ashley lay in bed, the blankets pulled up to her chin. When she had returned to the ranch house, Lucy had taken one look at her pale, drawn face and packed her off to bed. She was numb with fatigue, yet tense, unable to relax from the emotionally draining day.

Well, she thought, bigmouth that she was, she had gone and done it. She'd told Ryder Cantrell that she was in love with him. That had not been the swiftest move of her life. What kind of dimwit told a man who didn't love *her* that she loved *him*? Oh, well, it was done.

She rolled over and turned her thoughts to another matter. Ryder seemed almost obsessed with needing to hear time and again that she was going to stay by his side. It was as though he expected her to vanish into thin air at any moment. Why? Why was he so insecure? Perhaps it was because he was so weak and vulnerable at the moment, and saw himself as less than a whole man. His need for her now was deep, nearly frantic, but what would happen when he was well again? She just didn't know.

She did know that she loved him and always would. For the rest of her life she would love the Texan with the wide shoulders and fathomless green eyes.

At last she slept and dreamed of Ryder.

When Ashley, Lucy, and Pappy arrived at the hospital the next morning, Ryder was sitting up in bed, clean-shaven, sporting a slightly smaller bandage, and scowling.

"Oops. Not happy," Lucy said. "List your complaints in alphabetical order, brother dear."

"I hate this place."

"That's it?"

"They took my cigarettes. I need, want, *demand* to have my cigarettes."

"Hello," Ashley said, "my name is Ashley. I would like to kiss you good morning, but I can't because you are a motor mouth."

"Oh. Well, in that case I'll shut up. Come over here."

Ryder slid his hand to the nape of Ashley's neck and pulled her close, kissing her long and hard.

"Thank you," he said politely. "I needed that."

"You're welcome," she replied, not looking at Pappy, who was laughing merrily.

"I'm off to the condo site," Pappy said.

"Good." Ryder nodded. "Tell Hank I'm going to be pulling him off there later and putting him on the eminent-domain project."

"Yep." Pappy headed for the door.

"Lucy, verify the status of the remaining eminent-domain properties," Ryder ordered. "Make sure the checks have gone out."

"Yes, sir. Right away, sir. 'Bye, y'all." She and Pappy left.

"And me?" Ashley asked.

"You, woman, get in this bed!"

"No!"

"Damn."

The day was quiet and pleasant. Ryder slept more than he was awake, and Ashley spent her time sitting in the chair, wandering through the gift shop, and sipping strong coffee in the cafeteria. When Ryder awoke he made no mention of his pain, and Ashley withheld comment when she saw him clench his teeth or reach suddenly for his shoulder. She was occasionally shooed from the room by nurses wanting to take blood tests or to administer a shot to Ryder, and returned each time to find him crabby and swearing a blue streak.

They chatted about nothing of consequence and let comfortable silences fall. Ryder reached for her often, kissing her gently, stroking the palm of her hand, sifting his fingers through her heavy hair.

"You meant it, didn't you?" he said late that afternoon.

"Meant what?"

"You love me."

"Yes, Ryder, I do. Does that disturb you?"

"Would you understand if I said I wasn't going to dwell on it right now? Things are too off kilter. I need to get back on my feet, be who I was."

"I understand."

"It's going to take awhile for me to be the man you met, Ashley."

"It doesn't matter."

"We'll see," he said quietly.

"Ryder—"

"Lord, I'd kill for a cigarette. I really, really hate this place!"

*   *   *

The remainder of the week passed uneventfully, and each day had the same pattern. Lucy and Pappy came to the hospital in the morning to receive their daily instructions from Ryder and returned after work for a short visit. Ashley spent the entire day and part of the evening with Ryder, often having to be scolded by a nurse and told that visiting hours were over. Ryder's shoulder showed no sign of infection or other problem, and the bandage was reduced in size each time it was changed. He forced himself to move his left arm, often breaking out in a cold sweat from the pain the motion caused.

It was Ashley and Ryder's private world, where they smiled and kissed and argued endlessly over the fact that Ashley refused to sneak him in a pack of cigarettes.

On Saturday night Dr. Metcalf announced that Ryder could go home the next morning.

"Listen up, hotshot," the doctor said. "You can get dressed, walk around the ranch house until you're tired, and that's it. Do the same exercises you did two years ago for that shoulder. When the pain says stop, then stop. Any questions?"

"Yeah, I *was* wondering"—Ryder looked at Ashley—"if . . ."

"Probably," the doctor said, grinning. "As long as you don't get wild about it."

"Oh, dear me." Ashley blushed crimson.

Dr. Metcalf laughed. "Well," he asked. "I'm just trying to be helpful."

"Wonderful," she muttered.

"I mean it, Ryder," the doctor said, serious again. "You take it easy. There are just so many times I can glue you back together. Give that shoulder a chance to heal properly. I'll want to see you once a week for a while."

"Yeah. Hey, gotta cigarette?"

"Go home tomorrow. You will *not* be missed around here."

Ryder was half dressed when Pappy arrived the next morning to pick him up. Unable to move his arm enough to get it into the sleeve of his shirt, Ryder was not happy when Pappy entered the room.

"Just snap it around your chest," Pappy said, drawing the material closed.

"Where're Ashley and Lucy?"

"They're waiting at the ranch. Maria's gone to church with John, and the gals are fixin' a big lunch."

"Decent food. Unbelievable. Bring my cigarettes?"

"Yeah. You and Ashley spent a lot of time together this week. It's been good for both of you."

"It wasn't real, Pappy."

"The hell it wasn't, boy. This has been harsh reality, and that little girl didn't run for the hills. You put her through a harsh test, even though you didn't intend to, and, by gum, she stuck by you."

"It's not over yet. Hell, I can't even dress myself! Wait until she sees that someone has to cut my meat and—"

"And what? You won't be good enough for her anymore? Dammit, son, when are you going to let the past die? Why is Ashley paying a price for somethin' she had nothin' to do with? Think about the future, Ryder."

"No! You tell me one time the future turned out the way I planned. The last chance I gave it was Lucy and Jimmy and their baby. No, Pappy, no hopes, no dreams. Ashley is here now, but I sure as hell don't know if she will be tomorrow. I just don't know that."

"Oh, Ryder." Pappy sighed. "I wish . . . Well, let's go home."

* * *

Ryder kissed Ashley deeply when he entered the ranch house, and she was careful not to bump his shoulder.

"Lunch is ready," she said, smiling up at him.

"Jell-O?"

"Of course."

"I'm leaving."

The conversation was lively during lunch, and Ashley didn't stop her chatter as she reached over and cut Ryder's steak into bite-sized pieces. Pappy cleared his throat noisily, but Ryder refused to look in the old man's direction.

"Very good, and I thank you," Ryder said when he had finished and lit a cigarette.

"It's time you rested," Pappy said.

"Yeah, I'm tired." He stood up. "I'll sack out for a while."

"That's strange," Lucy said as Ryder left the room. "He didn't argue, just went off for his nap like a nice little boy."

"Wasn't quite the reaction I expected," Pappy agreed. "Why don't you go talk to him a bit, Ashley?"

"Well . . ."

"His room is at the end of the hall. I'll help Lucy with these dishes."

"All right, thank you." Ashley hurried from the room. Her cheeks were pink with embarrassment, and she knew it. That she and Ryder were lovers was no secret in that household, but everyone was so blasé about it. So there she was, trekking down the hall to Ryder's bedroom just as calm as you please, as though she were an old hand at this stuff.

The door was closed, and Ashley hesitated a moment before knocking lightly.

"Yeah?"

"Ryder, it's Ashley. May I come in?"

"Yeah, sure."

She stepped into the room and closed the door behind her. Her gaze swept over the enormous bedroom and its heavy wood furniture. Dark draperies had been pulled over the windows, making the room dim. She moved to the king-sized bed, where Ryder was stretched out on top of a chocolate-brown spread.

"Are you all right?" she asked.

"Just tired," he said, extending his hand to her. "Come on up here."

"I might hurt your shoulder."

"Lie on this side."

Ashley removed her shoes and lay down next to Ryder. A soft sigh escaped from her lips as she settled close to his body.

"You feel so good," she said softly. "I've missed being close to you like this."

"I missed you too," he said, turning his head to rest his lips on her forehead. "It's been a helluva week."

"You're home now, Ryder."

"And I'll bet you're uncomfortable being in here, with Pappy and Lucy roaming around outside."

"I'll get used to it."

"What's one more sacrifice, huh?" he said tightly.

"What do you mean?"

"Forget it. I don't feel like going over the whole list."

"Ryder, would you prefer to be alone? I don't seem to be doing much for your mood."

"Don't patronize me, Ashley!"

"I think I'll see you later," she said, starting to move off the bed.

"No, wait. I'm sorry. Stay here, okay?"

"Have you finished barking at me?" she asked, sliding back close to him.

"I apologize. None of this is your fault. I guess you'll . . . uh . . . want to start looking for a job pretty quickly."

"Are you trying to get rid of me?" she asked with a smile.

"Well, sitting around watching me sit around is not very exciting. You'll be bored out of your mind. I can't expect your life to come to a halt just because mine has. Our relationship has changed, because I'm not who I was before."

"Ryder, for heaven's sake, what is this all about? You act as though you're not going to recover, yet you know you are. You're the only one who's impatient about it. The time will pass. You'll have exercises to do to strengthen your shoulder and—"

"And you can cut up my meat. Ah, hell, this is ridiculous. Find a job, Ashley. Get on with your life."

"Quit feeling sorry for yourself! Take a nap. You're really crabby."

"Unsnap my shirt, will you? It's pulling too tightly across my chest."

She carefully undid the snaps on the shirt, brushing the material away from the bandage on Ryder's shoulder. Her heart quickened at the sight of his broad chest, at the mass of tawny curls, at the heat emanating from his body. On impulse she leaned over and kissed the taut, moist skin, her tongue drawing a lazy circle in the damp hair.

Ryder slid his hand to the nape of her neck and urged her upward to meet his lips. He kissed her hungrily, and she stretched out along his right side, returning the kiss in total abandonment.

"Ashley." He moaned. "I want you. I need to make love to you."

"But—"

"Let me love you, babe," he said, slowly lifting his left arm and placing it around her.

Ashley gazed into Ryder's eyes and saw the desire there, the need. He seemed to be hardly breathing as he waited for her reply, and a flicker of uncertainty crossed his face. A part of her felt compelled to tell him it was too soon, that he should rest, not chance hurting himself. But, no, she thought, this was Ryder, who stood his ground and gave no quarter. Stubborn Ryder, whom she loved with every fiber of her being. She had no right to pass judgment on his actions, and she would not.

"Yes," she said softly. "I want you too. I'll lock the door."

She slipped off the bed, walked across the room, and quietly locked the door. She shed her clothing and draped her things over a chair as Ryder rid himself of his own. She glanced anxiously at his face as he returned to the bed, her eyes searching for a signal of pain.

"Don't hover over me, Ashley," he said, frowning deeply. "I'm not a cripple."

"I know that. Still, I can't help but worry."

"Don't. Just don't. I feel as though you're waiting for me to fall short, to fail to meet your standards."

"Ryder, no!" she protested, lying down next to him. "I love you and I'm concerned about you, that's all. Lucy and Pappy are, too, but you seem to resent *my* caring."

"It's not that I resent it, I— Forget it." He claimed her mouth in a sensual kiss that brought her soaring instantly to a fever pitch of passion.

Ryder supported his weight on his right side and tentatively moved his left hand over Ashley's body. His caresses slowly became stronger, and when his lips followed the path blazed by his hand, Ashley whispered his name with longing.

"I want you so much," he said, his voice strained.

"Yes," she said, hardly able to breathe.

Ryder prepared himself, then lay back down. He put his arm around Ashley's waist and pulled her on top of him.

"Ryder?"

"Trust me, babe. It'll be fantastic. I can't support my weight on my arm, and I'd crush you."

With softly spoken words, he instructed her with loving patience, settling her over his thrusting manhood and bringing a gasp of surprise and pleasure from her lips. They moved as one and soared away until Ashley called to him to keep her from floating into oblivion. She collapsed onto his chest, wonderfully exhausted, and he shifted her sideways so that they lay spent in each other's arms.

"Oh, my," she said finally.

"Where there's a will, there's a way," he said, chuckling. "You were fantastic."

"I have to ask if you're all right."

"Good as new. Fully recovered. Fit as a—"

"Shut up."

"Right."

Within minutes Ryder was asleep. Ashley covered him with the spread and dressed, then quietly left the room. She hurried down the hall to her bedroom and brushed the tangles from her hair. Her mind was racing as she pressed her fingertips to her temples and stared out the window at the rolling fields.

Ryder was edgy, and she felt as though she were walking on eggs around him. He seemed determined to prove to her that he was a man in every sense of the word, and became cross when she expressed concern for him. One minute he was almost panicked in his need to have her near, and in the next was urging her to find a job and get on with her life. What did he really want from her? She sensed that the tension within him was building, and she felt as though she were with a time bomb.

With a frown, Ashley walked back into the kitchen. There was a note there saying that Lucy had gone into Houston and would not be home for dinner, and that Pappy had ridden to a neighboring ranch with John and Maria to look at several horses for sale.

Ashley wandered from room to room, bored and restless. She grew increasingly depressed as the hours passed and she went over in her mind the things Ryder had said. He was shouting to her in whispers, she was certain of it, but this time she didn't understand the message. Would he be more comfortable if she weren't around, seeing him physically impaired? Or would he feel that she had deserted him, in a way, if she searched for a job and found a focus other than him for her days? Oh, damn, he was a complicated man.

Pappy returned, and a short time later Ryder appeared in the living room, having managed to get his arm into the sleeve of his shirt. He kissed Ashley on the forehead, then listened as Pappy talked to him about whether to purchase the horses he'd seen.

"Do whatever you want," Ryder said, sinking onto the sofa next to Ashley. "I don't care."

"It's your money," Pappy said.

"If you want the horses, get 'em." Ryder shut his eyes and leaned his head back.

"You could go over and take a look at 'em," Pappy suggested.

"I said I don't care." Ryder spoke sharply, lifting his head to frown at Pappy.

"Got a burr under your saddle, boy?" Pappy asked calmly.

"I'm sorry," Ryder said. "I think I'll go for a walk. I need to stretch my legs."

He pushed himself to his feet and strode from the

room without looking at Ashley. Tears burned at the back of her eyes, and she blinked several times before looking at Pappy.

"I don't know what to do," she said softly. "I love him, Pappy, but I don't understand what he needs. He says he wants me with him, but then he tells me I should find a job."

"Patience, missy."

"I'm trying, but shouldn't I be able to make him happy?"

"Ryder needs to find inner peace first."

"And if he doesn't?"

"Give him some time. But don't lose track of yourself, either. You can't live your life entirely for another person. If you think it's time to look for work, then do it. If not, wait awhile. Ryder has to take care of himself a bit, too, you know. He's hurtin', that boy. Not just his body, but his mind and soul. His heart, too, I'd guess. Yep, patience is the word."

Ryder leaned against the stall and stared down at the kittens, who were tumbling over one another in the hay. His shoulder throbbed and ached, and he absently placed his hand on it.

He shouldn't have jumped all over Pappy about the horses, he thought. And he should have asked Ashley to come on the walk with him, instead of leaving the room without speaking to her. He should have done a lot of things differently, but it was too late to change them. Too late to stop loving Ashley. Too late for anything, except to be wide open for the hurt when she left him. She had felt so wonderful when he'd made love to her. She was all woman, and his. For now. Ashley was everything he had ever wanted, but those kinds of dreams never came true for him. So, loving Ashley was a mistake.

"Ah, hell," he said aloud, "why can't I love her, have her with me forever? Dammit, why do I always lose?"

Ashley stood at the kitchen window and watched as Ryder walked slowly back to the house. He was so big, so strong, she thought. She adored the way he walked. She did, in fact, love everything about Ryder Cantrell. She didn't always like his temper and those damnable walls he'd built around himself, or his mood swings, but she did love him. Patience, Pappy said. Patience and love. Would it be enough? Did she really, *really* have a future with Ryder?

"Hi," he said when he entered the kitchen. He pulled her into his arms.

"Hi." She tilted her head back to receive his kiss.

"Ashley," he said after he'd finally released her, "we're moving back into town tomorrow."

"What? Why?"

"I'm too restless out here. I'd rather go to the apartment. Then you'll be able to look for work more easily, too."

"I see," she said quietly. "Yes, I guess I had better get my future plans organized."

"Yeah. I'm going to go talk to Pappy about those horses."

"All right." Oh, dear heaven, he *did* want her to get on with her life, she thought frantically. A life . . . without him? He was taking her back into the city, away from his ranch, which was his private place, his sanctuary. Inch by inch their world was crumbling into dust, and soon she would have nothing.

Pappy looked up when Ryder came into the living room.

"Pappy," Ryder said, "Ashley and I are going back to the apartment tomorrow."

"Oh?"

"I can rest and exercise there just as easily, and she'll be able to look for work."

"Is that what she wants to do?"

"She has a future to think of, her career to be concerned about. I can't ask her to sit around with me while I'm laid up."

"You're pushin' her out of your life, boy. You lose her, you'll have no one to blame but yourself."

"I'm protecting myself, dammit!"

"Fine, you do that. Just keep on runnin' and don't stop for anyone. But, son, one of these days you're goin' to realize just how alone you are."

Ryder opened his mouth to speak, then closed it. He walked to the window and stared out of it, but didn't see anything. His shoulders slumped, and he bent his head as a silence fell over the room.

A cacophony of voices screamed in Ryder's mind as the ugly ghosts of the past demanded his attention. But from the depths of the din he heard a whisper, a name.

Ashley.

Nine

Ryder lifted his arm for the one hundred and twenty-fifth time, his hand tightly gripping the figure-eight weighted metal. Perspiration stood out on his brow as he clenched his teeth and counted on and on.

"One-fifty," he finally gasped, and halted the rigorous and painful ordeal.

He would rest, then begin again, as he had every day for the past week, since he and Ashley had returned to the apartment from the ranch. The stitches had been removed from his shoulder, and now it was up to him to rebuild the torn muscles and be the man he had been before.

One week in that apartment and he was going straight out of his mind.

It wasn't just the solitude and his impatience with his weakened body, it was also Ashley. Ashley, who was there, but wasn't. She came to him each night, eager for his touch, eager to love him, yet

166 of JOAN ELLIOTT PICKART

hardly spoke when they ate their meals or sat in the living room in the evenings. She went out each day in search of a job, told him, when she returned, about the applications she had filled out but said little about her hopes or plans. They were existing, not living, and Ryder grew more tense by the hour, waiting to hear the words, waiting for Ashley to say she was leaving him.

Ashley pulled the key from her purse and hesitated before inserting it in the lock. She had filled out another job application, which it would take all of five seconds to tell Ryder about, and then the silence would fall. Each day when she came back to the apartment she braced herself, expecting him to tell her to leave. At first she had welcomed his silence, but now it screamed at her, mocked her, made her grow more tense and edgy. The silence seemed like the ticking of a clock that surely measured the time she had left with the man she loved.

"Hello," she said, entering the living room and closing the door. "How did your exercises go?"

"Okay. Any luck?"

"Just another application."

"Well, something will turn up."

"I went by the office to see Lucy. She said she was disappointed we didn't come out to the ranch over the weekend."

"I didn't feel like it."

"So you said. Ryder, wouldn't you like to get out of here for a change of scenery? We could go out to dinner."

"No, I'd rather not."

"Why?"

"I said no, Ashley!"

"Dammit," she yelled, "what if *I* want to go out to dinner? What if *I* wanted to go to the ranch? All you do is sit there exercising, as if you're training for the

Olympics, and never talk, or ask me what I'd like to do."

"So go to a fancy restaurant! And visit the damn ranch! I'm trying to put my body back together. I thought you understood that."

"I do, Ryder, but what's the rush? What big plans do you have for when you're completely well? It's as though we're in limbo, living in a time warp. Exactly what are you so eager to do later that is keeping us from enjoying what we have now?"

"I might ask you the same thing, Ashley. Where will you be when your patient is healed?"

"What do you mean?" she whispered.

"You tell me," he said, pushing himself to his feet. "You've hardly said a dozen words all week. What's wrong? Afraid I'll have a relapse if you lay it on me too soon?"

"What are you talking about?"

"Ah, hell, give me a break. I'm not stupid, Ashley. You signed on when I was a healthy, complete man. I could take care of you physically, sexually, everything. Oh, I can perform in bed now, but out on the street if someone hassled you? No way. Your flaky Josh could knock me over. I'm not passing the test anymore, am I? I didn't live up to all the promises I made to you."

"That's not true! This isn't a contest, Ryder. Whose tests are you trying to pass? I don't understand any of this. I love you. I've told you that over and over, but I don't think it means anything to you. To me, love is forever, and—"

"Dammit, don't say forever to me." Ryder's jaw tightened. "Don't say that word."

"Don't say forever?" she asked, distressed. "Then what are we doing together, Ryder? What is it we're trying to prove? I know you don't love me, but I thought that at least we had some kind of future together. I was willing to accept you with your walls and secrets. I listened, really listened, to your whispers. You don't want any of it, do you? Not the todays with me or the tomorrows."

"Ashley—"

"I can't stay here anymore. I'm lonely. Lonely when I'm in the same room with you, because you're building the walls around yourself higher and stronger. I really hate to be lonely."

Ryder stared at Ashley, every muscle in his body tight, his heart racing, seeming to pound against his chest. She was leaving him. The moment had come, the one he had been expecting. And it hurt. It hurt with a greater intensity than he had expected it would. He wouldn't let her go! Hell, how could he stop her? She was lonely? With him? Dammit, what did she want from him? Forever. She wanted him to believe in hopes and dreams and fantasies, and he couldn't do that!

Ashley watched the emotions that were crossing Ryder's face, saw the haunting pain in the depth of his green eyes. Her mind screamed at him to reach out and pull her into his strong embrace, to tell her not to go, to stay and build a life with him . . . forever. But he wouldn't, because he didn't love her. She had lost the battle against the miscreant foes that had forced him to hide behind his walls and keep his secrets. And so she must go. With an ache in her heart and a love that would never die, she would walk away from Ryder Cantrell.

Swallowing the sob in her throat, she crossed the room to the bedroom and packed a suitcase. She'd return later for the rest of her things, but now she had to leave quickly, before she fell apart, before she begged Ryder to open the doors around his heart and soul and let her enter.

When she returned to the living room, Ryder was

staring out the window. She saw the rigid stance, the tight set to his shoulders. She saw her man, her love, her life, and tears spilled over onto her cheeks.

"Good-bye, Ryder," she said softly. "I do love you. I just wish . . . Good-bye."

Ryder didn't move or speak. He stood with his back to her, as though she were no longer there, and with a sob she rushed to the door and left him.

The sound of the door closing caused Ryder to spin around as panic swept over him.

"Ashley?" he said, his voice choked. "I love you. I do, babe! I just didn't know how to love you so you'd be happy. I failed. Dammit, I failed again, and I lost you." It was like every time before when he'd fallen short of being what was expected of him. Damn her! He hadn't been good enough to suit her, so she'd walked out. But had he tried to keep her, to bring sunshine into her life? he asked himself. Or had he decided at the onset that they would never make it and then sat back and waited for the end to come? Was it his fault?

Ashley, his lady, was gone. Ashley, with her ebony hair and lilting laughter, her little-girl smile and womanly passions, was gone. That proved that loving her had been a mistake. Yes, dammit, it did. But how he loved her, ached for her, and missed her, even though it had only been moments since she had walked out that door. She'd left him, but was it his fault? Had he made the biggest mistake of his life?

"It's too late, so what difference does it make?" Ryder said to the empty room. "It's over. Ah, Ashley!"

Ten

"There you are, sir," Ashley said, handing the vase to the man. "I'm sure your wife will enjoy them."

"I hope so. I want to surprise her."

"Is it a special occasion?"

"Nope, I just love her." He touched his fingers to the rim of his Stetson and left the flower shop.

Ashley rested her elbows on the counter and cupped her chin in her hands. What a dear, sweet, romantic cowboy, she thought. He loved his wife and was glad to say so.

"Lucky woman," she said aloud. No, darn it, she thought, she wasn't going to start thinking about Ryder and end up feeling sorry for herself. Surely the pain would start to ebb soon and time would soothe the ache in her heart. One month had passed since she had left Ryder's apartment. It had crept by with agonizing slowness. Four weeks of crying herself to sleep and wishing it all could have turned out differently. Thirty days and nights of knowing she would love Ryder for the rest of her life. If only some of the pain would lessen.

She had returned to Ryder's the next day to collect the remainder of her things, and had been grateful he was not there. Where he had gone she had no idea, as she had not been able to get him to budge from the apartment except to keep an appointment with Dr. Metcalf. She had stood in the bedroom and stared at the bed, remembering the exquisite lovemaking she had shared with Ryder. Then she had wandered from room to room, feeling masochistic, but not caring, as she touched Ryder's things, drank in his lingering scent, and allowed the tears to flow unchecked down her cheeks.

She had accepted the first job offered to her, which was in a florist's shop, and rented a small apartment. After she had tracked down Josh at the ever-famous Debbie Mary Sue's, he had helped her move the furniture from the warehouse into her new quarters. Josh had somehow known it was not the time for an I-told-you-so about Ryder Cantrell and was blessedly silent.

Ashley had telephoned Lucy and explained the situation. Lucy had called Ryder a dozen colorful names and had actually made Ashley smile.

As the bell over the door of the florist's shop jingled, Ashley snapped herself out of her gloomy reverie and forced a plastic smile on her face to greet the customer.

"Lucy," she said in surprise when she saw who it was.

"Hi, Ashley. I know we agreed to have lunch together next week, but I had to talk to you."

"What's wrong?"

"It's Ryder. Oh, damn him, he's acting like such a fool."

"Lucy, what's happened to him?" Ashley asked, her heart racing with fear.

"Nothing yet, but it will. He's working like a crazy man. He's been in Austin, troubleshooting, for the last ten days, and now he's taking over the eminent-domain contract himself. He won't listen to me, Pappy, the doctor. I'm worried sick about him."

"But why are you telling me this? There's nothing I can do."

"Ashley, please, go see him, talk to him. Someone has got to make him slow down before he does permanent damage to his shoulder and arm. He's drowning himself in his work, and there's only one reason for it. You."

"But—"

"He's at the site, down the block from your warehouse. Please, Ashley. I've got to get back to the office. Good-bye."

"Lucy, wait. I can't—"

"Please! He needs you."

Ashley pressed her hands to her burning cheeks as Lucy rushed out of the shop. This was crazy! she thought. Lucy wanted *her* to go see Ryder and convince him not to work so hard? That was totally insane. She hadn't even seen Ryder in a month. Why should he listen to her? But, dear Lord, what was he doing to himself? When they were together, all he'd been able to think about was recovering completely from his surgery. Didn't he care now that he could damage himself permanently? And Lucy was wrong, very wrong. Ashley knew it wasn't because of her. Ryder had allowed her to leave without a glance in her direction. He had made no attempt to contact her.

"I'm back," the woman who owned the shop said as she walked in. "Off you go to lunch, Ashley. Goodness, are you all right? You're awfully pale."

"What? Oh, yes, I'm fine. I'll see you in an hour."

"Take your time. You worked late again last night."

"Okay." Ashley grabbed her purse and went out the door.

She maneuvered the van through the surging Houston traffic and shook her head slightly in amazement. She was going to do it! She was actually on her way to see Ryder Cantrell and give him a piece of her mind. She was angry, rip-roaring mad, that he was placing himself in jeopardy and causing Lucy and Pappy needless distress. And she was scared. Scared to death that the moment she saw Ryder she would fall apart, come unglued, cry a bucket of tears, and make a fool of herself. No! she told herself firmly. She absolutely would not! She'd tell him to quit acting like an idiot, and that would be that. She owed it to Lucy and Pappy at least to try. Ryder probably wouldn't even listen to anything she said. If she had half a brain she'd turn around and drive back to the shop.

"So much for my brain," she said aloud as her old neighborhood came into view. "I'm a hopeless case."

The entire block had been fenced with chain link, and near the corner was a trailer similar to the one at the condominium site. Ashley parked on the street and walked through a small opening in the fence, spotting Pappy an instant later.

"Pappy," she called, hurrying toward him.

"Howdy, missy. Mighty good to see you."

"Lucy talked to me about Ryder. I really don't think he'll listen to me. In fact, this whole thing is ridiculous. Ryder doesn't care about me and certainly won't take my advice about his health."

"We'll see. He's hell-bent on destroyin' himself, it seems. Ever since he lost you, missy, he's been pushin', goin' at a pace that he's got no business keepin'. He's havin' a mighty hard time livin' with himself."

"Oh, Pappy, I didn't want to leave him. I love him so much. But I couldn't stay any longer."

"I know, missy. I'm not blamin' you one bit. That boy is stubborn and headstrong, and stupid at times. He's also the finest man in the state of Texas. Just a little more patience. A little more for your old Pappy, here, huh? Go talk to him."

Ashley sighed. "All right. But it won't do any good. Where is he?"

"In the trailer."

She nodded and took a deep breath, then tilted her chin determinedly and marched across the dusty expanse. The door to the trailer was open, and she could hear the low rumble of men's voices within. She went up the three wooden steps and entered. Ryder had his back to her and was talking to three other men.

Ashley immediately forgot why she was there as she gazed hungrily at Ryder. Her Ryder. Beautiful, warm, loving Ryder. There were his wide shoulders in the western shirt, the faded jeans hugging his hips and backside and thighs, the Stetson resting on the back of his head, where it no doubt had been pushed by his thumb. Ryder.

"Cantrell," she said, hoping, praying, her voice was steady. "I want to talk to you."

"Some gal wants you, Ryder," a man said.

"Yeah, in a minute," Ryder said, not turning.

"Cantrell!" Ashley yelled.

Ryder spun around, shock on his face. His gaze swept over her slender figure as if he couldn't believe what he was seeing. "Ashley? What are you—"

"I would like a word with you, Cantrell," she said stiffly. "Alone." Oh, dear heaven, she thought, she loved him so much. He looked so tired, and he was thinner. And she wanted to rush into his arms.

"Uh, yeah." There was a frown on his handsome face. "You guys take off for now." Ashley was here? he thought. She looked so pretty, cute, adorable. He wanted to kiss her, hold her.

"Sure, boss," he heard one of the men say. "Move your butts, boys. Ryder has personal business here."

The men walked out of the trailer, the last one shutting the door behind him. Ryder took off his Stetson, raked his hand through his hair, and replaced the hat with a firm tug.

"Ashley, I—" he started.

"Don't talk, just listen," she ordered, planting her hands on her hips. "I knew you were stubborn, but I didn't know you were selfish and uncaring."

"What?"

"Quiet! Just who do you think you are, Cantrell? What gives you the right to upset Lucy and Pappy by working yourself to death? They witnessed that horrible accident two years ago, sat in the waiting room for hours six weeks ago, praying you would be all right. And for what? What? To see you kill yourself by inches? Damn you, Cantrell! You are so loved by so many, and you only think of yourself."

"My name is Ryder," he said quietly.

"Shut up! Okay, so you don't believe in forever. That's your right, but this is the here and now, and you're putting Lucy and Pappy and me— No, cancel me. I don't have any part in this. You're putting them through living hell, and that is stinky and rotten. Come out from behind your walls for a minute and see what you're doing. Take a good look at yourself, Ryder Cantrell!"

"I—"

"Good-bye!" she said, marching to the door.

"Wait a minute!"

"Stuff it!"

She slammed the door with such force that Ryder jerked in surprise. He blinked once, as if not quite believing what had taken place. Then a slow smile tugged at the corners of his mouth and widened into a grin.

"Oh, yes, Ashley Hunt," he said, "I do love you. And I really don't think that is a mistake after all."

Ashley stomped across the lot and glowered at Pappy as she passed him.

"I love him," she said, without halting. "With every breath in my body, I love him." She climbed into her van and sped away.

He smiled. "Yep."

"Pappy!" Ryder yelled from the trailer door.

"I hear ya, son."

"Pappy," Ryder said, covering the distance between them in long strides, "call Lucy. Tell her to get Hank over here from the condo site. I want him to take charge of this job."

"Where you headed?"

"Hey, I'm not a well man, remember?" He chuckled. "I, Pappy, am going home to take a nap."

"Sounds good, boy."

"And, Pappy? I'm sorry, okay?"

"Yep. So? Now what?"

"I love her, Pappy," Ryder said quietly. "Now I pray she'll forgive me. I want to forget the past and look to the future. I want . . . forever."

"Bless you, son," Pappy said, clearing his throat. "You've been fightin' battles all your life, and this is the most important one you've ever taken on. Tell her, Ryder. Tell Ashley the whole story and be done with it once and for all. And then, son, tell her you love her."

"What if I'm too late, Pappy?" he asked, his voice choked.

"Go home. Rest."

"Yeah. See ya."

"Yep."

Ashley slowly climbed the stairs to her second-floor apartment, already dreading the long evening hours stretching before her. The afternoon had dragged by, with the image of Ryder Cantrell dancing continually before her eyes.

She shouldn't have gone to see him, she thought. All it had done was to deepen her pain, make her long even more to be held in his strong embrace, kissed and caressed, and carried into oblivion as they became one. She loved him, missed him, needed him. He was her life and he was lost to her for all time. She had her forever. Its name was loneliness.

She inserted her key in the door and stepped inside the small living room. She closed the door and leaned against it, shutting her eyes. A sudden noise in the room brought her instantly alert, and her eyes widened when she saw a box sitting on the sofa. Edging forward, she cautiously peered inside, and a gasp escaped from her lips.

It was her kitten.

The fuzzy bundle of black fur with white ears yawned, then curled up in a ball and fell asleep.

"She's yours," a deep voice said, "and she's ready to come home."

"Ryder!" Ashley exclaimed, her heart racing as she spun around and saw him standing in the doorway to her bedroom. "What are . . . How did—"

"Lucy gave me your address, and I picked your lock."

"You what?"

"I know how to do that," he said quietly, "and how to defend myself with my fists and a knife. I

learned it all, Ashley, along with how to hate, an
how not to trust anyone. I gave up on forevers an
dreams, and took whatever I could see right in fro
of me that I knew was real. I built a wall arour
myself that no one could get through. No one un
you, Ashley."

"What are you saying?" she asked, sinking on
the sofa, as her trembling legs refused to hold her.

"Where do I start?" he said, taking a deep breatl
"The beginning? The kid growing up in Dallas wh
saw his father drunk more often than sober? Yeah
suppose that's the place. That's why I hated thos
drugs in the hospital. I never want to lose control
my mind and body the way my father did. I saw it a
My mother's heart being slowly broken, Lucy growir
up in squalor because there was never any mone
But I had a plan, a way to fix it all."

"What do you mean?"

"When I was thirteen I made up my mind I wou
take care of my mother and Lucy. I told my mothe
promised her that I would be strong, protect he
work hard, and give her what she deserved. I g
after-school jobs and did anything I could find on tl
weekends. But it wasn't good enough. Somehow
failed, because my mother . . ."

He stopped speaking, and Ashley saw again th
haunting pain in the depths of his eyes. She clutche
her hands tightly in her lap, willing herself not
move, not to run to him and comfort him.

"My mother," he continued, his voice straine
"passed judgment on my father and me, and he wo
I came home from work one night and they we
gone. Gone. Lucy was sitting there all alone, cryin
and our parents . . . were gone."

"Oh, Ryder," Ashley said, wiping a tear off h
cheek.

"There was a note from my mother, saying sl

had to take care of my father and that she'd called an agency to tell them about Lucy and me. I'd tried so hard, worked so hard, and it hadn't been enough. Social workers came for us and put us in foster homes. I was angry, so full of hurt and confusion, and I never seemed to fit in with the families I was sent to live with. I never measured up, and they'd ship me someplace else. On the weekends I'd hitch-hike across town to see Lucy, to tell her to hang in there until I could find a way for us to be together."

"You were so young, Ryder. It must have been awful."

"I wasn't young for long. I ended up in a foster home in a rough neighborhood, where the people were in it for the money. I got beat to a pulp on the streets, and then I learned to defend myself any way I could. I got bigger, stronger, and scared the hell out of anyone who messed with me. I stole stuff, fenced it, stashed the money, and waited for the day when I could go get Lucy and be free of it all. I hated it—the fights, the constant feeling of failure, of never being what I was supposed to be. I hated it all. I gave up believing in dreams . . . and forevers."

"What finally happened?"

"One night the father in the house where I lived came home drunk. Something just snapped, I guess, because I went crazy, seeing him like that. I started hitting him, and it took three people to pull me off. I ran away, hid out in a deserted store, and then went for Lucy. I waited outside her school, and she came with me, no questions asked. I was seventeen then, and she was ten. I brought her here to Houston."

"And then?" Ashley asked, hardly breathing.

"I stole a gun."

"Oh, Ryder!"

He shrugged. "My money was gone. I put Lucy under a tree and told her not to move. Then I went to a small cabin and kicked in the back door. There I stood, pointing a gun at the kindest, most wonderful man I've ever known."

"Pappy."

"Yeah. He never blinked an eye. He just looked up at me and said, 'Son, dinner is about ready, so you might as well pull up a chair.' I'll never forget that moment as long as I live."

"And you stayed with him?"

"Yes. He took us in, gave us a home. . . . He never passed judgment on me. Never. I worked in construction for several years, made foreman. Later I gathered the best men I could find and started my own company. The rest you know. I made lots of money, bought the ranch for Pappy and Lucy. But, Ashley, the hate, the wariness, was so deep within me, and I couldn't trust anyone besides Lucy and Pappy. Then Jimmy and I became friends and—and I failed again. I didn't hold on to him when he needed me, and he died. That was the last of the dreams. Jimmy, Lucy, and their baby were real, were . . . forever, and it was shattered."

"It wasn't your fault that Jimmy died!"

"I know that, deep inside myself. But it was as though it were another warning not to go after elusive fantasies. I lived for the day, the hour, the minute I was existing in. Until you, babe."

"But you didn't let me get close to you, Ryder."

"I was too frightened," he said, drawing a shaky breath. "I was scared to death of loving you and even more afraid of losing you. You seemed so honest and real. But a part of me was waiting, watching for the signals of judgment, censure, the clues that would say I hadn't made the grade. I took your love and gave you nothing in return. I destroyed everything we had. I threw away our future, our forever, because of my past. Ashley, I—I— Ashley . . ."

"Ryder, shout it! Don't whisper the message and make me struggle to hear it. Please, Ryder!"

"Ashley, I love you! Oh, God, yes! I do love you so very much!"

And then she was in his arms.

Ryder crushed her to him, burying his face in her hair and holding her as if he would never let her go again. They clung to each other, not moving, scarcely breathing, and time seemed to stand still. Their strength, warmth, their very essences merged, wrapping them in a mindless daze as the past was pushed to the edge of oblivion and forgotten. Ryder slowly lifted his head, and Ashley gazed up at him. Their tears were mirrored in each other's eyes. The message they both saw did not have to be shouted or whispered, for it was crystal-clear. It was love. It was the future. It was forever. It was theirs.

"I love you, Ryder," Ashley said.

"And I love you. Ashley, will—will you marry me?"

"Oh, yes. Yes, I will. In fact, I have no choice."

"What?"

"The kitten. I'm not allowed to have pets here."

"Oh." He smiled. "Well, that's a logical reason for marrying me. To have a home for your cat."

"Oh, Ryder, I missed you so much. You are my world, my life."

"Ah, Ashley." He covered her mouth in a sensual kiss.

Ashley molded against him as their tongues met and their desires soared. She relished the feel of Ryder's arousal, announcing his want and need for her.

"I want you so much," he murmured into her hair. "I want to make love to you, but I'm not prepared."

"Are you saying I could get pregnant?"

"You could."

"Would you mind if I did?" she asked, smiling up

at him. "The kitten would have someone to play with."

"You'd have my baby, Ashley?" he asked, his voice low.

"With loving pride."

With a throaty moan, Ryder lifted her into his arms and carried her into the bedroom.

"Your shoulder!" she said.

"Is doing fine. Trust me."

"I do. Oh, Ryder, I do trust you, with everything that is mine to give."

Their lovemaking was ecstasy. It was tantalizing kisses and feathery touches. It was rediscovering the mysteries of one body that was so hard and taut, and another that was velvet-soft. They chanted each other's names, whispered endearments, and declared their love as their passions soared to a fever pitch. It was the coming together of a man and woman in love, who held the secret wish that their union would create a new life that would bring them immeasurable joy. It was heaven.

Afterward they lay close, holding on to each other as heartbeats quieted. Ryder sifted his fingers through Ashley's hair and drew it forward to cover her breasts.

"Ashley," he said quietly, "there's a building out at the ranch that could be converted into what you need for raising your plants. You could operate it on any scale you wanted to when I give you a break from being pregnant. We could build our own house out there, too, and raise our kids outside of the city. What do you think?"

"It sounds perfect. Wonderful. Pappy will be our children's grandfather, and teach them so much."

"Like hearing the shout of whispers?"

"Yes."

"Pappy gave me a great deal, Ashley. But you are giving what I never thought I'd have."

"What's that?"

"Forever. Forever, my love."

She smiled. "That's right, Cantrell."

"The name," he said, lowering his lips to hers, "is Ryder."

Ashley stood at the window and watched Ryder walk toward the house with his special lazy gait that was so much him. The Texas sky was a spectacle of color as the last streaks of the sunset transformed it into vibrant hues of purple, orange, and yellow.

In a moment she would be complete, for Ryder would pull her into his strong embrace and kiss her until she trembled. The walls around his heart and soul were gone. He was hers, and he loved her.

Suddenly she gasped, her hands coming to rest on her protruding stomach, and then she smiled. Tonight, she thought, their child would be born. A new Cantrell would walk tall and strong in Texas and wear the name with pride.

Cantrell. Ryder. Her love.

Forever.

THE EDITOR'S CORNER

We have four festive, touching LOVESWEPTs to complement the varied aspects of the glorious holiday season coming up.

First, remember what romance and fun you found in Joan Bramsch's **THE LIGHT SIDE** (LOVESWEPT #81)? And, especially, do you remember Sky's best friend and house mate, that magnificent model, Hooker Jablonski? Well, great news! Joan has given Hooker his very own love story ... **THE STALLION MAN**, LOVESWEPT #119. And for her modern day Romeo, Hooker, Joan has provided the perfect heroine in Juliet McLane. Juliet's a music teacher and musician ... and a "most practical lady." And it certainly isn't practical for a woman to fall for her fantasy lover! Hooker must teach the teacher a few lessons about the difference between image and reality ... and that he most definitely is flesh-and-blood reality! You'll relish this warm romance from talented Joan Bramsch.

How many times I've told you in our Editor's Corner about our great pleasure in finding and presenting a brand new romance writer. That is such a genuine sentiment shared by all of us at LOVESWEPT. So it is with much delight that we publish next month Hertha Schulze's first love story, **BEFORE AND AFTER**, LOVESWEPT #120. And what a debut book this is! Heroine Libby Carstairs is a little pudgy, a little dowdy, and a heck of a brainy Ph.D. student. Hero Blake Faulkner is a very worldly, very successful fashion photographer, and one heck of a man! He makes a reckless wager with a pompous make-up artist that he can turn Libby into a cover girl in just a few short weeks. Mildly insulted, but intrigued, Libby goes along with the bet ... then she begins to fall for the devastating Blake and the gambol turns serious. We think you're going to adore this thoroughly charming and chuckle-filled Pygmalion-type romance! And what a nifty, heartwarming twist it takes at the end!

TEMPEST, LOVESWEPT #121, marks the return to our list of the much loved Helen Mittermeyer. With her characteristic verve and storytelling force Helen gives us

(continued)

the passionate love story of Sage and Ross Tempest, whose love affair throughout their marriage has been stormy (which may even be putting it mildly). And, as always, you can count on Helen to enhance her romance with the endearing elements, as well as the downright funny ones that make her such a popular author. You'll long remember little Pip and Tad, not just Sage and Ross . . . and one very special, very naughty turkey!

A SUMMER SMILE, LOVESWEPT #122, by Iris Johansen is guaranteed to warm your heart and soul no matter how blustery the day is next month when you read it. Iris brings together two of her wonderfully memorable characters for their own bold, exciting love story. Daniel Seifert—remember Beau's captain in **BLUE VELVET**?— is given a hair-raising assignment to rescue a young woman from terrorists. She is Zilah, whom David took under his wing (**TOUCH THE HORIZON**) and helped to heal. Sparks fly—literally and figuratively—between this unlikely couple as they flee through the desert to safety in Sedikhan. Yet, learning Zilah's tragic secret, Daniel is frozen with fear . . . fear that only **A SUMMER SMILE** can melt. Oh, what a romantic reading experience this is!

All of us at LOVESWEPT wish you the happiest of holiday seasons.

Sincerely,

Carolyn Nichols

Carolyn Nichols
   Editor
LOVESWEPT
Bantam Books, Inc.
666 Fifth Avenue
New York, NY 10103

P.S. In case you forgot to send in your questionnaire last month, we're running it again on the next page. We'd really appreciate it if you could take the time and trouble to fill it out and return it to us.

Dear Reader:

As you know, our goal is to give you a "keeper" with every love story we publish. In our view a "keeper" blends the traditional beloved elements of a romance with truly original ingredients of characterization or plot or setting. Breaking new ground can be risky, but it's well worth it when one succeeds. We hope we succeed almost all the time. Now, well on the road to our third anniversary, we would appreciate a progress report from you. Please take a moment to let us know how you think we're doing.

1. Overall the quality of our stories has *improved* ☐
                                        declined ☐
                                 remained the same ☐

2. Would you trust us to increase the number of books we publish each month without sacrificing quality?   *yes* ☐   *no* ☐

3. How many romances do you buy each month? _____

4. Which romance brands do you regularly read?
    _____
    _____
    _____
    _____
    _____
    _____

            I choose my books by author, not brand name ☐

5. Please list your three favorite authors from other lines:

6. Please list your six favorite LOVESWEPT authors:

7. Would you be interested in buying reprinted editions of your favorite LOVESWEPT authors' romances published in the early months of the line?

8. Is there a special message you have for us? (Attach a page, if necessary.)

With our thanks to you for taking the time and trouble to respond,

Sincerely,

Carolyn Nichols

Valentina—she's a beauty, an enigma, a warm,
sensitive woman, a screen idol . . . goddess.

GODDESS

By Margaret Pemberton

There was a sound of laughter, of glasses clink-
ing. A sense of excitement so deep it nearly
took her breath away, seized her. With glowing
eyes Valentina stepped into the noise and heat
of the party.

"Lilli wants to meet you," a girl with a
friendly smile said, grabbing hold of Valentina's
hand and tugging her into the throng. "I'm
Patsy Smythe. Have you met Lilli before?"

"No," Daisy said, avoiding the apprecia-
tive touch of a strange male hand.

Patsy grinned. "Just treat her as if she's the
Queen of Sheba and you won't go far wrong.

Oh, someone has spilled rum on my skirt. How do you get rum stains out of chiffon?''

Valentina didn't know. Her gaze met Lilli Rainer's. Lilli's eyes were small and piercing, raisin-black in a powdered white face. She had been talking volubly, a long jade cigarette holder stabbing the air to emphasize her remarks. Now she halted, her anecdote forgotten. She had lived and breathed for the camera. Only talkies had defeated her. Her voice held the guttural tones of her native Germany and no amount of elocution lessons had been able to eradicate them. She had retired gracefully, allowing nobody to know of her bitter frustration. On seeing Valentina, she rose imperiously to her feet. No star or starlet from Worldwide Studios had been invited to the party. She did not like to be outshone and the girl before her, with her effortless grace and dark, fathom-deep eyes was doing just that. Everyone had turned in her direction as Patsy Smythe had led her across the room.

Lilli's carmine-painted lips tightened. "This is not a studio party," she said icily. "Admittance is by invitation only."

Valentina smiled. "I've been invited," she said pleasantly. "I came with Bob Kelly."

Lilli sat down slowly and gestured away those surrounding them. The amethyst satin dress Valentina wore was pathetically cheap and yet it looked marvelous on the girl. A spasm of jealousy caught at her aged throat and was gone. It was only the second rate that she could not tolerate. And the girl in front of her was far from second rate. "Do you work at Worldwide?" she asked sharply.

"No."

"Then you ought to," Lilli said tersely, "It's a first-rate studio and it has one of the best directors in town." She drew on her cigarette, inhaling deeply. "Where is Bob going to take you? Warner Brothers? Universal?"

"Not to any one of them," Valentina said composedly, not allowing her inner emotions to show. "Bob doesn't want me to work at the studios."

Lilli blew a wreath of smoke into the air and stared at her. "Then he's a fool," she said tartly. "You belong in front of the cameras. Anyone with half an eye can see that."

Noise rose and ebbed about them. Neither of them heard it.

"I know," Valentina said sharply and with breathtaking candor. "But Bob doesn't. Not yet."

Lilli crushed her cigarette out viciously. "And how long are you going to wait until he wakes up to reality? Whose life are you leading? Yours or his?" She leaned forward, grasping hold of Valentina's wrist, her eyes brilliant.

"There are very few, my child, a very tiny few, who can be instantly beloved by the cameras. It's nothing that can be learned. It's something you are born with. It's in here . . ." She stabbed at her head with a lacquered fingernail, "and in here . . ." She slapped her hand across her corseted stomach. "It's *inside* you. It's not actions and gestures, it's something that is innate." She released Valentina's wrist and leaned back in her chair. "And you have it."

Valentina could feel her heart beating in short, sharp strokes. Lilli was telling her what she already knew, and it was almost more than she could bear.

She had to get away. She needed peace and quiet in order to be able to think clearly. To still the unsettling emotions Lilli's words had aroused.

She fought her way from the crowded room into the ornate entrance hall. A chandelier hung brilliantly above her head; the carpet was wine-red, the walls covered in silk. There was a marble telephone stand and a dark, carved wooden chair beside it. She sat down, her legs trembling as if she were on the edge of an abyss. Someone had left cigarettes and a lighter on the telephone table. Clumsily she spilled them from their pack, picking one up, struggling with the lighter.

"Allow me," a deep-timbred voice said from the shadows of the stairs. The lighter clattered to the table, the cigarette dropped from her fingers as she whirled her head round.

He had been sitting on the stairs, just out of range of the chandelier's brilliance. Now he moved, rising to his feet, walking toward her with the athletic ease and sexual negligence of a natural born predator.

She couldn't speak, couldn't move. He withdrew a black Sobrainie from a gold cigarette case, lit it, inhaling deeply and then removed the cigarette from his mouth and set it gently between her lips.

She was shaking. Over the abyss and falling. Falling as Vidal Rakoczi softly murmured her name.

Goddess

*   *   *

There was still noise. Laughter and music were still loud in nearby rooms but Valentina was oblivious to it. She was aware of nothing but the dark, magnetic face staring down at her, the eyes pinning her in place, consuming her like dry tinder in a forest fire. She tried to stand, to gather some semblance of dignity, but could do neither. The wine-red of the walls and carpet, the brilliance of the chandelier, all spun around her in a dizzy vortex of light and color and in the center, drawing her like a moth to a flame, were the burning eyes of Vidal Rakoczi. She was suffocating, unable to breathe, to draw air into her lungs. The cigarette fell from her lips, scorching the amethyst satin. Swiftly he swept it from her knees, crushing it beneath his foot.

"Are you hurt?" The depth of feeling in his voice shocked her into mobility.

"I . . . No . . ." Unsteadily she rose to her feet. He made no movement to stand aside, to allow her to pass.

He was so close that she could feel the warmth of his breath on her cheek, smell the indefinable aroma of his maleness.

"Will you excuse me?" she asked, a pulse beating wildly in her throat.

"No." The gravity in his voice held her transfixed. His eyes had narrowed. They were bold and black and blatantly determined. "Now that I have found you again, I shall never excuse you to leave me. Not ever."

She felt herself sway and his hand grasped her arm, steadying her.

"Let's go where we can talk."

"No," she whispered, suddenly terrified as her dreams took on reality. She tried to pull away from him but he held her easily.

"Why not?" A black brow rose questioningly.

The touch of his hand seared her flesh. She could not go with him. To go with him would be to abandon Bob and that was unthinkable. He had done nothing to deserve such disloyalty. He had been kind to her. Kinder than anyone else had ever been. Sobs choked her throat. She loved Bob, but not in the way that he needed her to love him. The day would have come when she would have had to tell him so . . . but it hadn't come, and she couldn't just leave with Rakoczi. Not like this.

"No," she said again, her lips dry, her mouth parched. "Please let me go."

The strong, olive-toned hand tightened on her arm and the earth seemed to tremble beneath her feet. It was as if the very foundations upon which she had built her life since leaving the convent were cracking and crumbling around her. She made one last, valiant attempt to cling to the world that had been her haven.

"I came with Bob Kelly," she said, knowing even as she spoke that her battle was lost. "He will be looking for me."

A slight smile curved the corners of his mouth. "But he won't find you," he said. With devastating assurance he took her hand, and the course of her life changed.

Goddess

She wasn't aware of leaving the house. She wasn't aware of anything but Vidal Rakoczi's hand tightly imprisoning hers as she ran to keep up with his swift stride.

She sat in silence at his side in his car, peace and contentment lost to her forever. Something long dormant had at last been released. A zest, a recklessness for life that caused the blood to pound along her veins, and her nerve ends to throb. Like had met like. She had known it instinctively the day he had stalked across to her on the studio lot. Now there was no going back. No acceptance of anything less than life with the man who was at her side.

The car crowned a dune and he braked and halted. In the moonlight the heaving Pacific was silk-black, the swelling waves breaking into surging foam on a crescent of firm white sand. The night breeze from the sea was salt-laden and chilly. He took off his dinner jacket and draped it around her shoulders as they slipped and slid down the dunes to the beach. She stepped out of her high-heeled sandals, raising her face to the breeze.

"It's very beautiful here. And very lonely."

"That's why I come."

They walked down along in silence for a while, the Pacific breakers creaming and running up the shoreline only inches from their feet.

"You know what it is I want of you, don't you?" he asked at last, and a shiver ran down her spine. Whatever it was, she would give it freely. "I want to film you. To see if the luminous quality you posess transfers to the screen."

Goddess

The moon slid out from behind a bank of clouds. He had expected lavish thanks; vows of eternal gratitude; a silly stream of nonsense about how she had always wanted to be a movie star. Instead she remained silent, her face strangely serene. There was an inner stillness to her that he found profoundly refreshing. He picked up a pebble and skimmed it far out into the night black sea.

"I am a man of instincts," he said, stating a fact that no one who had come into contact with him would deny. "I believe that you have a rare gift, Valentina." Their hands touched fleetingly and she trembled. "I expect complete obedience. Absolute discipline."

His brows were pulled close together, his silhouetted face that of a Roman emperor accustomed to wielding total power. He halted, staring down at her. "Do you understand?"

Her head barely reached his shoulder. She turned her face up to his, the sea-breeze fanning her hair softly against her cheeks. The moonlight accentuated the breath-taking purity of her cheekbone and jaw line.

"Yes," she said, and at her composure his eyes gleamed with amusement.

"Where the devil did you spring from?" he asked, a smile touching his mouth.

Her eyes sparkled in the darkness as she said with steely determination. "Wherever i was, I'm not going back."

He began to laugh and as he did so she stumbled, falling against him. His arms closed around her, steadying her. For a second they remained motionless and then the laughter faded from his eyes and he lowered his head, his mouth claiming hers in swift, sure contact.

Nothing had prepared her for Vidal's kiss. Her lips trembled and then parted willingly beneath his. There was sudden shock and an onrush of pleasure as his tongue sought and demanded hers, setting her on fire.

LOVESWEPT

Love Stories you'll never forget by authors you'll always remember

☐	21603	**Heaven's Price #1** Sandra Brown	$1.95
☐	21604	**Surrender #2** Helen Mittermeyer	$1.95
☐	21600	**The Joining Stone #3** Noelle Berry McCue	$1.95
☐	21601	**Silver Miracles #4** Fayrene Preston	$1.95
☐	21605	**Matching Wits #5** Carla Neggers	$1.95
☐	21606	**A Love for All Time #6** Dorothy Garlock	$1.95
☐	21609	**Hard Drivin' Man #10** Nancy Carlson	$1.95
☐	21611	**Hunter's Payne #12** Joan J. Domning	$1.95
☐	21618	**Tiger Lady #13** Joan Domning	$1.95
☐	21614	**Brief Delight #15** Helen Mittermeyer	$1.95
☐	21639	**The Planting Season #33** Dorothy Garlock	$1.95
☐	21627	**The Trustworthy Redhead #35** Iris Johansen	$1.95

Prices and availability subject to change without notice.

Buy them at your local bookstore or use this handy coupon for ordering:

 # LOVESWEPT

Love Stories you'll never forget by authors you'll always remember

LOVESWEPT

Love Stories you'll never forget
by authors you'll always remember

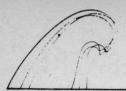

LOVESWEPT

*Love Stories you'll never forget
by authors you'll always remember*